Property of Granite Gate

Praise for the Novels of Cassie Edwards

"High adventure and a surprise season this Indian romance."
—Affaire de Coeur

"Edwards puts an emphasis on placing authentic customs and language in each book. Her Indian books have generated much interest throughout the country, and elsewhere."
—Journal Gazette (Mattoon, IL)

"Few can relate a story as well as Ms. Edwards."
—Midwest Book Review

"Edwards consistently gives the reader a strong love story, rich in Indian lore, filled with passion and memorable characters."
—Romantic Times

"Excellent . . . an endearing story . . . filled with heartwarming characters."
—Under the Covers

"A fine writer . . . accurate. . . . Indian history and language keep readers interested."
—Greeley Tribune (Greeley, CO)

"Captivating . . . heartwarming . . . beautiful . . . a winner."
—Rendezvous

"Edwards moves readers with love and compassion."
—Bell, Book & Candle

SWIFT HORSE

❖◆❖◆❖◆❖

Cassie Edwards

A SIGNET BOOK

SIGNET
Published by New American Library, a division of
Penguin Group (USA) Inc., 375 Hudson Street,
New York, New York 10014, USA
Penguin Group (Canada), 90 Eglinton Avenue East, Suite 700, Toronto,
Ontario M4P 2Y3, Canada (a division of Pearson Penguin Canada Inc.)
Penguin Books Ltd., 80 Strand, London WC2R 0RL, England
Penguin Ireland, 25 St. Stephen's Green, Dublin 2,
Ireland (a division of Penguin Books Ltd.)
Penguin Group (Australia), 250 Camberwell Road, Camberwell, Victoria 3124,
Australia (a division of Pearson Australia Group Pty. Ltd.)
Penguin Books India Pvt. Ltd., 11 Community Centre, Panchsheel Park,
New Delhi - 110 017, India
Penguin Group (NZ), cnr Airborne and Rosedale Roads, Albany,
Auckland 1310, New Zealand (a division of Pearson New Zealand Ltd.)
Penguin Books (South Africa) (Pty.) Ltd., 24 Sturdee Avenue,
Rosebank, Johannesburg 2196, South Africa

Penguin Books Ltd., Registered Offices:
80 Strand, London WC2R 0RL, England

First published by Signet, an imprint of New American Library,
a division of Penguin Group (USA) Inc.

ISBN 0-7394-5960-0

In friendship, I dedicate *Swift Horse*
to Laura LaRocque of Dunseth, North Dakota.

Always,
Cassie Edwards

To the heat of the sun,
From the fires of hell,
Dreams of illusions,
Only I can tell.
Whispers of love,
Your shadow beyond,
Let me grow old,
Let me be strong,
Surrender into our passions,
Share secrets of pride,
Promises and persuasion,
Always kept inside.
I long to hold you,
Man of joy,
Embrace me forever,
Long for me to have and to hold,
Mist my eyes, till we grow old,
> *together forever.*
> > —Jacqueline Manson

Chapter 1

Kentucky, 1850
October, the Corn-ripening Moon

The four-room log cabin was being warmed by a slow-burning fire in the stone fireplace. Colorful blankets and plush pelts hung along the walls, while the aroma of venison stew cooking in a huge brass kettle filled the air. Midafternoon sunlight splashed a golden glow through the windows into the room.

Swift Horse, who was the *tyee*, chief, of the Wind Clan of the Creek tribe, sat in a wooden rocking chair before the fire. He slowly rocked as he discussed the upcoming hunt with his close friend One Eye, of the Wolf Clan of Creek, who sat in a second rocking chair a few feet away.

Soft Wind, Swift Horse's younger sister, sat on a blanket on the floor a short distance back from her brother and One Eye, preparing corn for the upcoming meal. Corn was her Creek people's main staple of food. Many delectable, nourishing dishes were made from it.

Soft Wind's face was beautiful, her body petite and clothed today in a prettily beaded doeskin dress and matching moccasins. She wore a ribbon woven into the lone braid that hung down her straight and narrow back, and a necklace of shells around her neck.

As the hum of voices between her brother and One Eye continued, Soft Wind held a wooden pestle as she ground corn in a deep, round wooden bowl.

But her mind was elsewhere.

It was on a man, another friend of her brother and their people. She was in love with Edward James Eveland, a white man who was the resident trading-post storekeeper at their village. She planned to marry Edward James soon.

Her clan approved of Edward James even though his skin was white, but she hadn't yet announced her marriage plans to anyone but her brother. Once she got the chore of telling One Eye behind her . . . then she could finally reveal her happy news to everyone!

She shifted the wooden bowl on her lap and paused as she gazed up at her brother, then moved her gaze slowly over to One Eye. She had been waiting for the opportune moment to tell One Eye of her wedding plans, yet dreaded telling him her news as well, for deep down she feared his reaction. He had never kept his intention to marry her a secret, and had long talked of her being his wife.

This was why she was going to break the news to him in the presence of her brother. If One Eye reacted as badly as she expected him to, surely her brother would finally see that he was not trustworthy.

Soft Wind saw a shiftiness about One Eye that her brother was blinded to. The look in his single eye reflected his behavior, and she couldn't understand how her brother, the astute person that he was, couldn't see this character flaw. It could only be that he just wouldn't let himself.

He and One Eye had been friends since they were young braves learning how to walk in the moccasins of a man. Both were now chiefs of their separate clans.

As Swift Horse and One Eye continued talking about the hunt, Soft Wind gazed at her brother again with admiration. He was a chief at his young age of twenty-six, and a man everyone

respected. He was so handsome today in his colorful beaded jacket, fringed buckskin breeches,
and moccasins. A wool sash was tied at his waist,
and a wide cloth headband, decorated only with
a feather, held his raven-black hair back from his
sculpted face.

Yes, he was handsome and noble, this brother
of hers, a man of much kindness and intelligence,
and a leader of leaders. Their father, who had
been chief before Swift Horse, had taught him
well. He'd died not long ago, at the hands of renegades, as had their mother.

Soft Wind gazed at Swift Horse's bold nose,
his high cheekbones, his full lips, and eyes that
blazed with intelligence. His sinewed muscles
made the seams of his jacket strain at his shoulders and arms.

She thought again of another man, the man
she loved. He was handsome, too, but in a different way. He was not as muscled, or as tall as
her brother, but his blue eyes had mystified her
the first time she had looked into them. His
warm, sincere smile had brought her into loving
him almost immediately.

When there was a slight pause in the conver-
sation between her brother and One Eye, Soft
Wind started to seize the opportunity to tell One
Eye about her decision to leave her personal

lodge, to move into another—a man's, whose bed she would share every night. But again the talk resumed about the hunt, and Soft Wind sighed to herself and resumed grinding the corn into a fine meal that she planned to use that evening.

The longer she waited, the more apprehensive she grew about telling One Eye at all. But if she didn't tell him personally, and he found out otherwise, it would truly anger him, and something told her that it was best not to anger him needlessly. So, she waited.

"I hope to find many *itchy-lako,* big deer, while on the upcoming hunt," Swift Horse said, studying One Eye.

He would never forget the bravery of his friend on the day he lost his eye. While hunting, they both had become trapped by a bear. One Eye, who had been called Lone Wolf until that day, had jumped the bear and sunk a knife into its heart, but not before the bear had injured one of his eyes so badly that it had to be removed. It was then that he had been renamed One Eye.

Yes, One Eye had gotten the scar on his face valiantly, and Swift Horse would forever be grateful, for the bear had lunged at Swift Horse and would have killed him immediately, had it not been for One Eye's courageous act. They had been ardent friends before that had happened, but now their bond was even stronger.

"But as we learned as young braves, the primary target of the upcoming hunt is the white-tailed *itchu*," Swift Horse said. "When winter arrives, the rutting season begins. It is a time when bucks become aggressive and they abandon the deep cover of the forest in the search for mates. The hunt will be even better then."

"But now is the time for our people's main trade," One Eye said, giving a quick glance toward Soft Wind, whom he had loved for so long, and so badly wanted to marry. Yet being so disfigured, he was afraid that when she looked at him, it was with secret disgust. Being as sweet as she was, however, she had always been careful not to reveal these feelings to him.

"There is also beaver, bear, and raccoon," Swift Horse said, having noticed how his friend had given Soft Wind a quick glance, and seen in his one eye a longing that he understood. Swift Horse knew that his friend pined over a woman he knew could never be his. He felt sure that One Eye was aware of Soft Wind's feelings for the white man who was admired by all Creek for his honesty in trading and his sincerity in how he felt about the red man.

But if One Eye wasn't aware of her feelings for Edward James, Swift Horse knew that he would know soon, for Soft Wind was going to tell One Eye about the upcoming nuptials today. He knew this to be so because he had seen it in her eyes today and in how she hesitated from time to time, seeming ready to say something.

Swift Horse had already accepted it inside his heart that he had lost his sister to this white man, but he was not sure yet how One Eye would take knowing how she felt for someone of another skin color. Swift Horse thought that One Eye blamed his disfigurement for her having turned away from him. But knowing his sister better than anyone else, Swift Horse knew that Soft Wind's heart was pure. She could never choose one man over another because one was no longer appealing in appearance.

"There is also less likelihood of meat spoilage in the colder months," One Eye said, sensing his friend's hesitation, and wondering why. It surely had something to do with Soft Wind because One Eye had seen Swift Horse give his sister occasional uneasy glances. He sensed something was different about Soft Wind today. She would look at them both as though she were ready to tell them something, then would return her gaze back to her chore at hand.

One Eye hated to hear what she surely would say even before this private council was over. He knew that Soft Wind loved another man, and it was rumored that soon there would be vows spoken between them. Now all that was needed was for Soft Wind to confirm it verbally.

One Eye was prepared not to let the truth tear at his being, for he had prepared himself even as far back as when he had lost his eye that things would never be the same for him in many respects, especially where women were concerned. Most looked away from him rather than linger their eyes on him with disgust in their depths.

"We are going to use fire this time to catch the whitetail deer," Swift Horse said. He turned his eyes to Soft Wind. "Sister, you must be sure to remind the other women not to go into the forest once the fires have been set, because they might get trapped."

"I will be sure to tell them," Soft Wind murmured. "They are aware of this practice of using fire since you use this means of hunting at least one time a year."

Unable to keep her feelings to herself any longer, Soft Wind dropped the wooden pestle into the bowl, stood up quickly, and said, "One

Eye, I have some news to tell you. I plan to marry Edward James Eveland soon," she blurted out.

One Eye flinched as though he had been hit, even though he had expected this announcement. It made him bitter to know that he was hideous to look at, while the young trader was handsome.

Swift Horse saw his friend's reaction and his sister's uneasiness over it. "Soft Wind, come to me," he said, rising and holding his hands out.

Feeling bad over seeing One Eye's pain, Soft Wind went to her brother and moved into his arms, welcoming them. When he embraced her, it was with comfort and love, which she needed so much.

"I am certain that One Eye is happy for you, my sister," Swift Horse said as he looked past her shoulder and into One Eye's one eye.

He could see a quiet bitterness and he understood. This man had adored Soft Wind since they were children. But she had never returned those feelings, and never could. She had even voiced negative feelings about One Eye. She saw him no longer as a friend her brother could trust.

She had told Swift Horse that since the day of the bear attack, she felt that One Eye had changed into someone else . . . someone very unlikable. Swift Horse had not seen that in his friend. He still trusted him and he would never forget the courage that it took for One Eye to go against that bear to save Swift Horse's life.

"It is time for me to share my news openly with everyone," Soft Wind said, gazing into her brother's midnight dark eyes.

"My little, beautiful sister, you have been sharing this with everyone for much longer than you seem to realize," Swift Horse said, gently taking her by the shoulders and holding her away from him as he still gazed into her luscious dark eyes that were shaded by thick lashes. "It has been in your voice when you talk. It has been in your eyes. Even when you walk, it is different. Yes, it will not be news to anyone, as I am certain it was not news to One Eye. But it will be good that you openly say it."

"Do they truly realize my feelings?" Soft Wind said, her eyes widening. "Am I that revealing in how I behave?"

"Yes," Swift Horse said, chuckling beneath his breath.

She smiled broadly. "Then I will reveal the truth to everyone," she said, then slid her eyes over to One Eye. "Besides my brother, you are the first, One Eye."

"I am happy for you," One Eye said thickly as

he slowly rose from the chair, then stood facing her and Swift Horse.

"Thank you for understanding. And One Eye, one day a woman will be announcing to her people that she will be taking you as a husband," Soft Wind said. Then she forced herself to say things she truly did not feel, but felt it was necessary. "You are a man of such kindness and heart," she murmured. "Yes, a woman is waiting out there for you somewhere. Your visions, your dreams, will lead you to her."

Surprising both Swift Horse and One Eye, Soft Wind stepped away from her brother and gave One Eye a hug, even though every fiber of her being abhorred the action. But she felt this was necessary, for the sake of her brother, who still saw One Eye as his dearest friend.

Swift Horse watched as One Eye, unsure of what to do, held his arms at his sides, then slowly brought them up and returned Soft Wind's hug.

"You have been my brother's best friend for so long, and a friend of our family. I wish you well and do hope that one day a woman will come into your life who will make your heart smile as mine is smiling now," Soft Wind murmured, hoping that her feelings of loathing at being in his arms were not visible to her brother, or One Eye. She was glad to be able to finally step away from him and return to her task of making meal from corn.

"Thank you for what you just did," One Eye said thickly as he gazed down at Soft Wind. He slowly sat down in the rocking chair as Swift Horse returned to his. "I shall remember your embrace and soft words, always."

Soft Wind forced a smile as she gazed up at him, then focused on her task at hand now that the terrible chore of telling One Eye was finally behind her. She had only a bit more preparation to go before she would be finished with this chore of preparing her corn and ready to begin her next.

She already had the main part of the evening meal, the meat and vegetables, cooking in the pot. After her brother and One Eye left the cabin, she would then begin preparing the bread.

Knowing that it was best to divert the talk away from his sister's upcoming nuptials, Swift Horse gazed over at One Eye and said, "I saw it in a vision that the hunt will be good for both your clan and ours."

Unable to quell her excitement at being so in love and soon to marry the man she adored, Soft Wind giggled and drew both her brother's and One Eye's attention back to her.

"I saw it in a vision that I was already Edward

James's wife," she blurted out. "In the vision I was enjoying living at his and his sister's home."

Soft Wind could not help but notice a look that came into her brother's eyes at the mention of Edward James's sister, Marsha, and knew that he, too, had fallen in love with someone of a different skin color. But he had not yet talked openly of this to anyone but Soft Wind.

"It was also in my vision about Marsha's tidiness," she then said. "She is so very tidy and neat."

Swift Horse laughed softly. "Yes, you will be able to relax in that respect while living with Edward James and his sister Marsha," he said. "You are neat and tidy, too—so much sometimes that I am afraid to step into this cabin with my moccasins on."

Soft Wind giggled. "Sometimes while I am at the trading post and watching people coming and going for trade, I sense that Marsha would like for them to remove their moccasins, too," she said, her eyes dancing. "For certain she has changed the neatness of Edward James's trading post. Everything is in its place."

"I had noticed the difference in the trading post and had suspected that the white woman was responsible," Swift Horse said. "There is suddenly a place for everything. I had even noticed the same color blankets lying together. . . ."

His words faded to nothing as he heard a commotion outside his lodge. He rose quickly to his feet and went to the door and opened it. His jaw tightened with anger when he saw two cows running through the village and then into the corn crop, trampling through it.

"Not again," Swift Horse groaned to himself.

"What is it, brother?" Soft Wind said as she, then One Eye, stepped outside with Swift Horse.

She followed the path of her brother's gaze, and saw the cows making their way through the corn crop, leaving so much destruction behind them.

"The cowkeeper's cows," Swift Horse said, doubling his hands into tight fists at his sides. "The cowkeeper has not heeded my warnings about allowing his cows to run loose."

"They come into my town, too, where they also trample and destroy our crops," One Eye said heatedly. "Come. We must kill them. Now!"

Swift Horse reached a hand out for One Eye, stopping him from going to his horse and grabbing a rifle from its gunboot. "No, not while they are in my village," he said tightly. "I cherish the lives of all animals unless they are needed for food for my people, or for clothes."

"What, then, will you do?" One Eye asked, his voice tight with anger.

"I will capture and take them to the cowkeeper, and again warn him," Swift Horse said, breaking away from One Eye and Soft Wind. He ran into the corn field, and with the help of two of his warriors, soon had a rope around the necks of the cows, and stopped them.

"Tie the cows behind my horse," Swift Horse said to the warrior.

"I will go with you," One Eye said, already mounting his own steed.

"It was my village that was wronged today, so I will go alone to again try to rectify it," Swift Horse said, swinging himself into his saddle made from a puma skin. He smiled at his sister. "I will be home in time to share the evening meal with you."

Soft Wind nodded. She watched her brother ride away from the town with the cows trailing behind him, then turned her eyes to One Eye, who was riding from the village.

Soft Wind went back inside and began cleaning up the mess she had made while making meal, wondering what her brother would say to the cowkeeper. He had been given that name by the Creek because of how many of these strange animals he owned.

And he not only owned cows, but also hogs that he kept in pens, and chickens that he allowed to roam as free as he did the cows.

She smiled when she thought of the many times she had found fresh eggs that had been left behind by the man's chickens. At least in that respect, she found something positive about the bare-headed, red-whiskered white man who came onto land that had at one time belonged solely to the Creek.

She thought again of her brother and his task at hand. She hoped that he made the cowkeeper understand the problem of allowing his animals to roam free, destroying what belonged to the Creek.

She didn't know what else might be needed to make him understand. She knew that her brother was a man who ruled with a peaceful heart, but even he could be pushed only so far.

Chapter 2

No more be grieved at that
which thou hast done.
—William Shakespeare

Swift Horse sat in his saddle as he gazed down at the tall, thin white man whose hair was gone, yet whose face was covered with a thick red beard.

"Take your cows," Swift Horse said flatly, his hand on the rifle in his gunboot. "But this is my last warning to you. Keep your cows from our crops, or else I—"

"Or else what?" Alan Burton, the cowkeeper, said, his right hand resting on a holstered pistol at his right side. "You don't own the land. It's free. My cows can run free, and you ain't gonna do nothin' about it or you'd have already tried."

He glared up at Swift Horse. "You're yeller through and through or else you *would* have done more than talk when you get so riled about my cows bein' where you say they shouldn't be."

Alan went and untied his cows from Swift Horse's horse, then waved his right hand in the direction of Swift Horse's village. "Get on with you, Injun," he snarled. "Go back to where you belong."

He started walking the cows toward a part of his land that he had fenced off for them, used only at milking time. He looked over his shoulder at Swift Horse. "Remember this, savage," he shouted. "This land *is* free. There ain't nothin' you can do about me—or my animals—being on it."

"You do not know the true interpretation of 'free,'" Swift Horse shouted back, watching Alan Burton walking away from him. "Let me explain some of the meaning to you, Cowkeeper. If you continue allowing your cows to run free and destroy my people's crops, you will soon know the true lack of freedom. You will lose the freedom of being able to enter our village to purchase supplies at the trading post. You will be a prisoner of your own making because there are no more trading posts in this area. You are at the mercy of this one that sits amidst my Creek village."

Alan stopped and turned and glared at Swift Horse. "Your threats mean nothing to me," he snarled. "I will go to Fort Hill and tell them that you threatened me."

"Go there," Swift Horse said with mischief in his eyes. "The soldiers there, under tho command of Colonel Harris, have been my people's ardent friends and allies since my Creek people helped the Americans against the British in the War of 1776."

Alan glowered, for he did feel alone, more than ever before since his move to Kentucky from Missouri. Not all that long ago his wife and children had been slain by a renegade. He hadn't found a woman to replace his wife, for there weren't any settlers close by who had unwed women among them.

Swift Horse wheeled his horse around and rode away, assured this time that he had gotten his point across and that he surely had nothing to be concerned about from the cowkeeper.

Chapter 3

My brain is wild,
My breath comes quick,
The blood is listening in my frame.
—Percy Bysshe Shelley

It was another autumn day, in which strange strings of cobwebs floated through the air, attaching themselves to anything and anybody.

Marsha Jane Eveland was fussing to herself as she removed some of those cobwebs from her long golden hair as she came into her cabin after hanging clothes on a line outside the back of her home. Sighing heavily to herself, she turned and looked around at the cabin that until recently had been occupied by only her older brother Edward James.

Upon her arrival, she had stepped into a masculine setting, but she had placed the pretty doilies that she had crocheted on the end tables and on the back and arms of the couch that sat before the fire. She had also placed braided rugs here and there on the oak floor, rugs that she had helped make with her mother while they had lived in Georgia.

"Mama," she whispered, a sob lodging in her throat at the remembrance of that horrible day when renegades had attacked the wagon that had carried her and her mother and father, as they had been traveling from Georgia to Kentucky. They had left the only home that Marsha had ever known to be near Edward James.

Her father, who had a strange crippling disease, no longer had the strength to keep up their farm, and had thought it best to get the family together again. Marsha knew that her father had agreed to the move for her mother's sake— "worry wart," her father had called her mother. Her mother hadn't been able to get Edward James off her mind from the moment he had left for Kentucky to be a storekeeper at a trading post established in an Indian village.

They had almost arrived at the Creek village when a band of renegades had attacked. Her parents had been killed immediately, but Marsha had managed to survive the attack when what was left of the cavalry, who had been escorting them to Kentucky, managed to chase off the attackers.

But before they fled, Marsha had seen the

one-eyed renegade who was solely responsible
for her parents' death. A shudder shook Marsha
when she recalled how often she had dreamed
of that man and how her dreams of him
haunted her.

She turned again and gazed into the rolling
flames of the fire as they caressed the huge
logs, her heart aching anew after recalling that
wretched day. Slowly she turned her eyes upward
and found herself gazing at herself in the large
mirror that hung above the mantel. It had belonged to her mother, and had originally hung
above the lovely mantel in their Georgia home.

How often had her mother brushed Marsha's
waist-length hair for her in front of that mirror as
she stood before the fire, warming herself before
her day's activities had begun? She lifted her
hand to her hair and ran her fingers through the
golden, thick tresses.

That day of the ambush, she had seen one
of the renegades gazing at her hair. She had, as
quickly, seen how he had yanked a knife from a
sheath at his right side. She knew what his intentions were, abhorred by even the thought of
being scalped by that evil red man.

She could hardly make out his features, for
they were marred by ungodly streaks of red and

black across his face. "War paint, I imagine," she whispered.

Just as he had let out a horrendous, mind-shattering war whoop and had begun making his way toward her, she heard the report of the gun that had downed that heartless man. Marsha would never forget how frightened she was. She couldn't move a muscle in her body!

She remembered how his knife dropped from his hand as he clawed at his bloody chest before falling from his horse, dead. One of the cavalrymen had downed the man, saving Marsha's life.

"I've changed since then," she whispered to herself, now slowly moving her hand over her facial features. Until that day, she had been so happy, so content with the world. But since then, she had found it hard to smile.

She doubted, now, how anyone could think she was pretty, for surely she wore her sadness on her face, and even in her violet eyes.

She tried not to. She knew that she had to move on with her life, but she just wasn't sure what that life was to include. For now, she was taking it a day at a time, caring for her brother and trying to put the past behind her.

Marsha went to a table and picked up her crochet work and sat down before the fire. She had worked hard all morning, washing and cleaning. It was now time for her to indulge herself before preparing the evening meal.

When she had first taken up her crochet work after having arrived at her brother's home, her fingers had shook too much to be able to hook the thread with the needle.

Finally, her fingers were no longer trembling, and she intended to make many more pretty things for her brother's cabin—even though she could see his look of "Oh, no, not something else lacy for my house" when he gazed at what she sat crocheting.

She only gave him a sweet smile, which usually would do the trick. Since she was a child, with an older brother to look after her, that smile had been able to win her anything from him.

And now?

Yes, when she smiled she could see how relieved it made him, not only because he had always loved her smile, but because he could tell that, day by day, she was getting past the tragedy and was finally becoming the sister he had always known, someone who was always there with a smile and comforting words when anyone had a bad day.

"Big brother, I will be all right," she whispered to herself as she looped thread around a finger, and then around the crochet hook.

She got lost now in thoughts of her brother. He had moved to Kentucky two years ago and had established a trading post at a Creek Indian village. The Creek people had seen that it was in their best interest to have a post in their village, for they didn't have to travel far to make their trade. Other clans came from far and wide to deliver their deerskins, furs, hides, tallow, oils, and honey to the trading post, knowing that her brother paid well for the supple hides.

Her brother had explained that trading with Indians was a lucrative business for him; that a traders' life followed seasonal rhythms linked to the autumn hunt. He had also said that he enjoyed having his post at the Creek village because he felt much safer surrounded by a peaceful Indian such as the Creek, instead of being at the mercy of those who killed whites for pleasure.

Again Marsha was reminded of that renegade who killed her parents, a man who not only had the one empty socket where his eye had once been, but also a livid white scar that ran down from the socket, across his right cheek.

Forcing this man from her mind again, she continued thinking about how things in her life were, now that she lived with her brother.

She had been there for one month now. Upon

her arrival, she had been surprised to see how different this Indian village was from others. She learned that the reason these people were called Creek was because their impressive towns lined the banks of beautiful creeks and streams.

She also found that instead of living in tepees, the Creek lived in cabins. The roofs of their cabins were shingled with bark. The sides were made of poles and sticks plastered with mud. Marsha had noticed that one of those cabins was larger than all of the others. Her brother had told her that it was occupied by the village chief, whose name was Swift Horse.

"Swift Horse," she whispered beneath her breath as she paused with her crocheting.

She smiled as she thought of this man and how he had greeted her on the day of her arrival at the village. His dark eyes had lingered on Marsha for a moment or two as her brother had introduced her to him; Chief Swift Horse was even more handsome than any white man she'd ever seen or known. He was broad-shouldered, muscled, and spoke with a gentle kindness.

But she had looked quickly away. She was confused by her attraction to the handsome chief. This was the last thing she would have ever imagined happening. She wanted to hate all Indians, not be infatuated by any. She kept reminding herself that her parents were dead *because* of Indians.

She hoped that her brother would change his mind soon and agree to return to Georgia. But as each day passed, she became more doubtful of that ever happening. He was enjoying mixing with the Indians, as well as others who came from other villages to trade with him, while she was filled with warring emotions!

How could she trust Indians—any of them?

How could her brother?

"I'll just keep on minding my own business as best I can," she murmured, resuming her crocheting.

Marsha paused again from her crocheting when she heard the drone of voices in the store of the trading post.

Her ears perked up when she heard a familiar soft, feminine voice. It was the voice of a Creek woman she now knew as Soft Wind, who was Chief Swift Horse's sister. She came often, and Marsha did not want to think about why she was there so much.

Could the maiden have fallen in love with Edward James? Was her brother in love with her?

"Well, by George, I will not put off asking about her any longer," Marsha whispered to herself as she again resumed her crocheting.

But the truth be known, she was afraid to hear her brother's answer.

On those days when she'd heard Soft Wind's voice, when Edward James came back to the living quarters, she could see a flush to his cheeks and something different about his blue eyes. She shuddered at the thought of his having fallen in love with Soft Wind.

On several occasions, when he had left for a lengthy period of time and without good reason, Marsha had begun to suspect that he was with a woman, but didn't ask. She was afraid to hear, for she knew of no close-by settlers, and her brother was not gone long enough to have traveled far to meet a lady. That had to mean that he had met someone in this village.

Marsha lay her crochet work aside, for she was aware of the sudden silence in the storeroom. That meant that Soft Wind had left. She hurried from the couch to the window and slowly drew aside the sheer curtain.

She saw a young, petite, beautiful maiden dressed in doeskin, her coal-black hair hanging in a lone braid down her back, walking away from the trading post with her brother Chief Swift Horse. Soft Wind's smile was so radiant that Marsha was afraid that it meant the maiden did have feelings for her brother.

Suddenly footsteps behind her drew Marsha quickly around. She found her brother there with the same sort of sappy look on his face that came with his having spent time with Soft Wind.

Smiling, he took her hands in his. "Sis, I have something to tell you," he said, searching her eyes.

Marsha's insides tightened, she was so afraid that her brother was going to tell her that he was in love with Soft Wind! Then she grew cold inside when he told her news even worse than what she had feared.

"Sis, I'm going to marry Soft Wind," Edward James said. "I'm going to marry her soon." His smile faded when Marsha yanked her hands free of his and took a quick step away from him.

"Edward James, how can you?" she gasped out. "How can you forget so easily that it was Indians who killed our parents? Edward, she . . . this pretty maiden Soft Wind . . . is Indian."

"I understand very well that she is Indian," Edward James said, taken aback by his sister's stunned behavior, for he suspected that she had to know about his feelings for Soft Wind for some time.

Marsha had seen him and Soft Wind together many times. They had taken long walks together, and Marsha had even seen them kissing one evening.

"Edward James, you are marrying this woman for all of the wrong reasons," Marsha blurted out.

"What do you mean?" Edward James said, forking an eyebrow. "What other reason than loving her can there be?"

"I see you doing this as a way to secure protection forever from her chieftain brother," Marsha said tightly. "Also, wouldn't her marriage to you work in the behalf of her own people? Wouldn't it be a way for her to be a source of information and advice for the chief? Wouldn't she gain access to, and be in control of, the stock of trade goods? Wouldn't it—"

Edward James grabbed Marsha gently by the shoulders. "Stop it. Where on earth did all of that come from?" he said tightly. "Say nothing more, especially something you might regret later. All that you just said has nothing to do with my reason for marrying Soft Wind, or her marrying me. We are in love. And . . . we don't want to wait any longer."

"I just can't believe it," Marsha said as she yanked herself free of his grip. "Edward James, I am aghast at what you are planning to do. Let me remind you that men of this woman's skin color murdered our parents in cold blood," Marsha said dryly, as the horrors of that day again flashed before her eyes.

"Sis, the murderer's blood is not of Soft Wind's blood," Edward James said thickly. "She is all purity and sweetness. Her brother is a kind and gentle leader of his people, someone I would trust with my own life. You must change your mind about this, for I am marrying the woman and she will be brought into our house."

That thought sent a cold chill down Marsha's spine, yet she knew that no matter what she said or did, her brother was going to marry this Indian maiden and she had no choice but to try to accept it.

"Marsha?" Edward James said, stepping closer and placing a gentle hand on her cheek. "Please say that you understand and will try to accept Soft Wind into your life. She will be my wife, Marsha. She will be your sister-in-law."

Marsha swallowed hard, then flung herself into her brother's arms. "I'll try," she sobbed. "Oh, Lord, big brother, I shall try my hardest to accept her into my life, yet . . . yet . . . it is so hard to forget that day, and that . . . that . . . Indians took so much from us."

"Renegades, sis," Edward James said, correcting her. "Renegades who have no heart or soul.

Just because they were Indian does not make all Indians bad!"

"I know," Marsha said, again thinking of the one Indian she could not remove from her mind, ever.

Swift Horse.

She knew that he was nothing like those who came out of the forest with death paint all over their faces. In time, she hoped to get to know Swift Horse better, which would be assured now that his sister was marrying Marsha's brother. That thought made her realize that perhaps what her brother was doing was not all that bad after all.

"You will be all right with this, won't you?" Edward James asked, gently holding Marsha away from him, his eyes gazing intensely into hers.

"Yes, I shall be all right," Marsha murmured, then again hugged him. "I'm sorry I've been someone foreign to you since my arrival to Kentucky. I'll try to be myself again."

"That will certainly be welcomed," Edward James said, chuckling. "Yep, that will certainly be welcomed, little sister."

Chapter 4

How calm it was!—the silence there
By such a chain was bound
That even the busy woodpecker
Made stiller by her sound
The inviolable quietness. . . .
                    —Percy Bysshe Shelley

Just as Swift Horse was about to leave his cabin for the morning council with his warriors, he stopped and listened.

There it was again.

His horses were restless and neighing. That had to mean that someone might be in, or near, his corral, for his horses were normally content, especially this early in the morning.

Even his sister wasn't at Swift Horse's cabin yet.

Most days she was up before Swift Horse, preparing their morning meal, but today's council about the cowkeeper was to be held at daybreak so that nothing would interfere with the council.

Although Swift Horse felt that he had finally

made the cowkeeper realize that he meant business about the cows, it was Alan Burton's belligerent manner that made Swift Horse think that there would more than likely still be confrontations with the red-whiskered man.

He believed that warnings did not mean all that much to the cowkeeper, and plans must be made to stop him, once and for all.

There!

He heard it again! The horses were growing more uneasy.

"Brother, what is causing the horses to make so much noise that it awakened me?" Soft Wind asked, walking into the cabin in her doeskin dress and moccasins, yawning and stretching her arms above her head.

Then she stopped and gazed in wonder at Swift Horse. "And why are you up so early?" she asked, forking an eyebrow. "What troubles you, brother? You are dressed already, which means that you had to have been dressed before the horses began making those unusual noises."

"An early council is planned to discuss the cowkeeper," Swift Horse said, looking past her and through a window.

He tensed up when he saw a movement outside just past his pole corral at the back of the cabin.

"What is it?" Soft Wind asked as she saw her brother's eyes narrow as he grabbed his rifle, which stood beside the door.

"Someone is out back," Swift Horse said, turning and opening the door. He looked at Soft Wind over his shoulder. "Lock the door behind me!"

Suddenly afraid, Soft Wind did as he said, then went to the window and gazed from it.

She was stunned when she saw a man with black skin limping toward Swift Horse's storage building at the back of the yard.

Soft Wind gasped and placed a hand to her mouth when she saw deep, bloody-looking scars on his bare back, and the look of horror on his face when he looked over his shoulder and saw Swift Horse running toward him, shouting, "Stop."

Chapter 5

I shut my eyes and turned them on my heart.
—Robert Browning

"Stop!" Swift Horse shouted again, cringing when he saw the terrible deep and bloody scars on the black man's bare back as he continued to limp toward the opened door of the storage shed.

"Do not be afraid," Swift Horse tried to reassure him. "You are among friends. My people do not have slaves. We do not believe in slavery!"

Swift Horse was aware of slave trading among whites, and he had heard of runaway slaves. Swift Horse concluded that this black man must have run away.

To Swift Horse all men were equal, whether their skin was white, black, or copper—even though he often saw the whites as inferior because of their ignorance of how things should be.

But his beloved mother had taught him when he was just a small brave, that even whites were human beings, although some were heartless in so many ways, especially toward anyone other than their own skin coloring.

And now he saw the true depths of their ignorance about black people.

He continued to run toward the limping man. Then suddenly the black man stopped.

He watched as the black man turned slowly around to face Swift Horse. Even though he must be in terrible pain and surely felt endangered, he showed that he was a man of dignity as he stood there with a lifted chin.

"I am a friend, someone you can trust," Swift Horse said again, in a friendly, hopefully reassuring, tone. Yet Swift Horse had never spoken to a black man before. He now wondered what language he spoke. Did blacks have their own language, as whites and redskins had their own?

Swift Horse could speak both English and Spanish. Perhaps he could learn this man's language, too, if needed.

"Do you understand me when I tell you that I am a friend?" Swift Horse asked, lowering his rifle to his side when he saw how the man's eyes darted back and forth between looking at the rifle and then at Swift Horse.

Swift Horse wanted to place the rifle on the ground to prove that he truly was a friend; but seeing how large the man was, with muscles bulging at his arms and shoulders, he knew that it was foolish to give him a chance to overpower him.

"I mean no one no harm," the man finally said in a deep sort of booming voice. "I'se just needs food, water, and rest, then I'se be on my way."

Swift Horse was relieved that the man finally spoke to him. Cautiously, he took a step closer to him. When the man still stood there, and did not assume a threatening stance, Swift Horse stepped close enough to touch him on the arm. He could feel the man tense beneath his touch, yet he still stood there, his eyes wide, his body tight.

"You have been terribly mistreated," Swift Horse said softly. "Can I see the wounds on your back more closely? There is someone among my people who can doctor them if you will allow it."

The man stood there, rigid, silently watching Swift Horse, then gave a gentle nod. Swift Horse turned him and gazed at the gashes on his back. When Swift Horse saw the depth of the raw, bloody scars, he cringed. He could tell that they had been inflicted more than a day or so ago, but still they were oozing blood.

He knew that they must be terribly painful, and did not want to think of how it must have been at the moment of impact by the whip, for he knew that was how those wounds had been inflicted. He had heard about how white slave owners used whips on their slaves, and it sickened him even to think about how this man had suffered from such mistreatment.

He stepped around and faced the man again. "What is your name?" he asked thickly, realizing just how wronged this man had been at the hands of whites, as so many red men had been wronged and killed by them.

"Abraham," the man said in an even deeper, huskier voice than moments ago. "My mama named me Abraham from a character in my mama's Bible."

Swift Horse was relieved to see that Abraham was obviously no longer afraid, but instead appeared to be grateful to be treated with a measure of respect and kindness, perhaps for the first time in his life.

"Abraham, how far have you traveled on your bare feet and with such injuries?" Swift Horse asked, touched deeply by this man who was large, yet seemed to be of gentle nature.

"I'se be from the tip of Southern Florida land, but I don't knows figures or distances, but I do knows I'se traveled far, so far it hurts me to even think 'bout goin' farther," Abraham said. "I fled a heartless mastah after my wife and baby son were killed by the man for bein' sickly and of no use to him anymores."

"I am so very sorry for your loss," Swift Horse said, suddenly reliving the deaths of his own parents at the hands of heartless renegades. Yes, there were evil men of all colors.

"Thank you," Abraham said, humbly lowering his eyes. Then he looked quickly at Swift Horse again. "My mastah has been known to pay much money fo' the return of escaped slaves. Will you return me to my mastah fo' payment?"

"I have heard that one captured runaway is worth a gun and three blankets to Indians who take runaways back to those who enslaved them. That is the equivalent of forty pounds of dressed deerskin," Swift Horse said, seeing how knowing this made Abraham stiffen and his eyes to mist with tears. "I know that some would turn you in for such valuables. But I will not do this thing against you. I am a man who cherishes freedom for all men of all colors."

A look of utter relief washed across Abraham's face. He gave Swift Horse a sudden, broad smile. "Thank youse, thank youse," he blurted out.

"Please let me stay with you. I'se be worth my keep."

Suddenly Abraham fell to his knees before Swift Horse. Tears streamed from his eyes as he gazed up at him. "I begs you to please lets me stay," he said, his voice breaking. "I'se good in the fields. I saw your crops. I'se can tend to dem."

Swift Horse hated to see such a big man lowered to begging, especially since only moments ago there was such pride in his stance.

He placed a gentle hand on Abraham's shoulder. "Please stand," he said, his own voice breaking. "And, yes, you can stay, but not as a slave, but as a *freed* man, a friend. When you are stronger and more able, you can help with the hunt alongside my warriors when they go on a hunt for deer or bear."

Abraham pushed himself up and stood tall before Swift Horse. "Thank youse," he said, smiling as he wiped away his tears. Then his smile faded and he openly became tense all over again. "If I am seen with youse, an Indian, won't whites retaliate agains' youse?"

"Whites do fear Indians and blacks interacting," Swift Horse said thickly. "But they will not interfere in my decision to keep you, a black man, at my village. I will protect you from any harm."

"But what if my mastah hunts and finds me?" Abraham said, visibly shuddering.

"Believe me when I say that I hate injustice— all injustices," Swift Horse said tightly. "Like I have promised, I will do what I can for you. And I know how far Florida land is from here, so I do not see your, as you call him, 'mastah' coming this far to find only one runaway slave. And slave owners here in Kentucky would not dare interfere in what I have done. They know that I have strong ties with the white authorities at Fort Hill and that the colonel there would stand up with me regarding any decision I make about anyone, or anything."

"You are so kind," Abraham said, again lowering his eyes. Then he looked up at Swift Horse again. "What Indian tribe are you a part of?" he asked. "In Florida land, there are many who are called Seminole. What are you called?"

"I am Chief Swift Horse of the Creek tribe," Swift Horse said, squaring his shoulders proudly.

"I am in the presence of a chief?" Abraham said, obviously in awe of knowing this.

"Yes, I am chief of my Wind Clan of Creek," Swift Horse said, smiling. Then his smile faded. "I am sorry about your treatment at the hands of whites. It was a whip that caused the deep scars on your back, was it not?"

"Yessah, it was a whip," Abraham said, his voice breaking. "My mastah whips all blacks to teach obedience. Abraham . . . could not be . . . obedient any longer."

Swift Horse turned when he heard footsteps approaching. He saw that it was his sister, who had obviously seen everything from his back window. She had gone for their village conjurer, who was also their people's shaman.

He turned and saw how Abraham seemed suddenly afraid again. Swift Horse placed a gentle, reassuring hand on the man's arm. "This is my people's shaman, who to you might be called a doctor, since you were a part of the white world and that is how they refer to their healers," he said. "His name is Bright Moon, and the woman is my sister Soft Wind."

Still Abraham stood stiffly, his eyes darting from Soft Wind to Bright Moon and then to Swift Horse.

"As I am your friend, so are Bright Moon and Soft Wind your friends," Swift Horse reassured. "Bright Moon would like to look at your wounds and study them so that he can know how to medicate them."

Bright Moon stepped up to Swift Horse's side

in his long robe with the paintings of many crescent moons on the buckskin. His gray hair was worn in one long braid down his back, and his old, dark eyes had lost much of their luster.

"Let him see you," Swift Horse again urged, taking one of Abraham's arms and slowly turning him so that his back was to him and Bright Moon.

The Shaman stepped closer and studied the bloody scars. "I have never seen anything like this before," he said in his perfect English. "Whoever did this to you must not have had a heart. The scars still ooze blood although I can see they are some days old."

Swift Horse saw many coming from their lodges, and realized that word had spread about the black man that had come into their village. He was amazed at how many were there, for the hour was early, when only women should be up and adding wood to their cook fires. Even children were there with their mothers and fathers. They tried to get closer to the man who had a skin color most of them had not seen before.

A small child stepped boldly up to Abraham as Abraham turned and saw so many people there, staring at him.

Abraham looked down at the small girl as she stepped up to him and ran a hand across his stomach, then looked at her fingers. Everyone was quiet as this was happening.

"Why does the black color not come off onto my hand?" the child asked. She gazed up without fear, but wonder, into Abraham's black eyes. "Is the color not painted onto your skin?"

Seeing how this might become embarrassing for Abraham, Swift Horse knelt down before the child, Pretty Star, and took her hand in his. "You do not see color on your skin from having touched this man because this color is his own, not painted," he explained patiently. "This man's skin is black like our own is copperred."

Pretty Star smiled at Swift Horse as he took his hand from hers, then ran back and stood between her mother and father.

Swift Horse smiled, for he was proud of his people's alertness and inquisitive nature. That was how people learned, even after they had reached the midpoint of their lives.

He explained all about Abraham, why he was there, and how badly he was injured.

"Bright Moon will take Abraham now to his personal lodge and help lead the black man on to the quick path of recovery," Swift Horse said, turning and smiling at Abraham, which seemed to help reassure him.

Swift Horse went up to Abraham. "It is all

right to go with my shaman to his lodge," he said. "He is an intelligent healer. When you leave his lodge, you will be without pain, and soon your back will heal only to scars that will surely be with you for the rest of your life. Perhaps it will be good that they will be there. They will remind you always of the cruelty of one man, while you are among those who are good—who are your friends, forever."

Suddenly Abraham flung himself into Swift Horse's arms, again thanking him, then stepped away from him and walked beside Bright Moon as everyone parted and made way for them to pass, then walked away themselves, to return to their homes and their duties of the day.

Soft Wind embraced Swift Horse. "You prove time and again how much a man of heart you are," she murmured. "I love you and am so proud of you."

"The man has suffered enough inhumanity," Swift Horse said, stepping away from Soft Wind. He took her hands in his. "My sister, there are so many injustices that you are not even aware of."

"I know," she murmured. "Yes, I know. I plan to listen well to my white husband as I have always listened to you. By doing that, I will feel safe enough against such tyrants who harmed Abraham so terribly."

"Yes, you will be safe as Edward James's wife, for you will have him *and* your brother to look after you then," he said, his thoughts wandering to someone else.

His sister would soon speak vows with Edward James Eveland. That meant he would get to see more of the beautiful, petite, golden-haired white woman who spent most of her days hidden away at the back of the trading post, where there were living quarters for her and her brother.

From the moment she had arrived at his village, he had only been able to see her a few times, and that was when she was at the trading-post store, helping her brother.

He had wanted to see her more often, even speak to her by name, yet thus far all that he had been able to do was get glances of her. But that had been enough to convince him that he wanted to know more about her, and be with her. He had not been able to get this woman off his mind from the moment he first saw her.

But he knew that she had been traumatized by people of his own skin coloring, when renegades had come out of nowhere and murdered her parents. He knew this because Edward James had explained the tragedy to Swift Horse when Swift

Horse had questioned him about this woman who seemed to be so sad and withdrawn.

After Swift Horse heard the story, something deep within him wanted to make things right for her again. Yet . . . again . . . there was the fact that his skin was the same color as those who had brought this sadness into her eyes.

Could she ever see beyond his red skin and know that he was not at all like the renegades? That he was a man of kindness and good heart who wanted nothing but good for those he loved?

Chapter 6

I regret little, I would
change still less.
—Robert Browning

The late-afternoon sun was twining its way through the multicolored autumn leaves. Marsha sat on a blanket beside her brother, who kept gazing at Soft Wind, who sat by her own brother's side in the center of a circle of people who had come from other villages to make plans for the upcoming hunt.

The council was usually held in the huge council house, but the day of this meeting being so lovely, it was being held outside, instead.

Marsha felt awkward being there. This was her first time participating in anything with the Creek, but she felt she had no choice when her brother told her that now that he was going to marry Soft Wind, Marsha must involve herself in Creek activities that ofttimes included him because he was the resident storekeeper of the trading post.

The day had been long and Marsha was weary. Her back ached as she tried so hard to sit there trying to look attentive while first one warrior and then another, spoke his mind about the hunt, as their chief and people sat listening.

But now the council was drawing to a close. Marsha knew this to be so, because Edward James had told her that when the village shaman, Bright Moon, sat down before his chief and performed some sort of ceremony, the council would soon be over.

Bright Moon was there now, taking several things that Marsha did not recognize from his buckskin bag. Her brother had said that when the shaman did this, he was preparing medicine for the purpose of attracting deer for his chief and those who would be participating in the upcoming hunt.

She now knew, too, how important the deerskin trade was to the Creek. Slowly she was learning the ways of the Creek, which she knew was important since she was living among them.

While Bright Moon continued making medicine as everyone sat mutely quiet and attentive around him, Marsha again became lost in thought. Since her parents' deaths, she had not wanted to mingle with any Indians, even though she was truly intrigued by Chief Swift Horse.

But today, for her brother's sake, she had had no choice but to do as he had asked. He had told her that everyone who was attending the council must think positive at all times, for it was said that any negative feelings felt by anyone would keep the deer away. Marsha tried not to look too bored, or too anxious for this meeting to be over. She especially tried not to think anything negative.

She had to confess to herself that she had enjoyed having the opportunity to have a closer look at Chief Swift Horse, who intrigued her more and more every time she saw him. But someone else had drawn her attention more than once this waning afternoon. She looked again at the black man.

She had seen him yesterday before he had been given clean clothes to wear. She knew how terribly scarred his back was. This evening he was standing at the back of the circle of people, his dark eyes wide as he watched the shaman preparing his special medicine.

She could tell that his intrigue of this shaman, and perhaps the Creek as a whole, was as great as was Marsha's of Swift Horse. She knew his name now. It was Abraham. And he was clothed today in clean, fringed buckskins, his shirt left open in front to keep the material loose from his back so that his injuries there would heal better.

He wore no bandages, but she knew that he had been doctored by Bright Moon, and that was surely why Abraham watched the elderly conjurer so intensely. It was apparent that he believed in the man now. He also seemed to be comfortable with the Creek, a people who had not only offered him kindness, but also a home.

She had seen him taken to a vacant cabin at the edge of town, which he now made his residence, and had watched several Creek women coming and going from the cabin, taking food, blankets, and furniture. She would never forget the look of awe in Abraham's dark eyes as he had watched the procession of women bringing things to him.

It was apparent that during his lifetime he had never had anything of his own, nor anyone to treat him with even a measure of kindness.

As Abraham sat slowly down on the blanket that one of the women had given to him, Marsha turned her eyes away. She did not want him to catch her staring at him, even though she could hardly help it. She was in total dismay at how he had made his way so far from where he had been a slave. He had traveled even farther than

Marsha, and she had found the journey grueling at times even though she had the comforts of a wagon.

He had traveled the full distance on his bare feet and with a back that had been terribly mutilated by those who claimed him as theirs.

It touched her heart deeply that Swift Horse had taken Abraham in and had vowed to protect him from any more harm.

This proved, too, that these Creek people were vastly different from those who had taken her parents' lives. The renegades' lives were centered around murdering and maiming and wreaking havoc wherever they could get away with doing it.

She prayed often to herself that they would never make their way here, to this Creek village. She would hate to see things change from how they were now, a place where Marsha was finally beginning to feel at ease and at peace with herself. She knew how important this was since her brother was going to be bringing a Creek woman into their home, to stay.

She thought again about why the shaman was making medicine. For the deer hunt. Again she thought about the importance of not allowing anything negative into the village that might harm their hunt.

She had to wonder if Abraham's mere presence, or her own, might bring something negative to the hunt. They were both new to the Creek.

She had noticed how some of the Creek people had looked over their shoulders more than once at Abraham, and some even at her. That had made her uneasy, for she could not help but think that those few might see both her and Abraham as an interference in their lives at a time when all should be calm and normal, and perhaps a danger to their livelihood—to their hunt.

She made herself forget those thoughts, for she knew that her brother was loved by everyone there, so surely they saw her as someone who was as kind and warm as well. She had spent as little time at the store as possible, going there only when her brother asked for her help. Otherwise, she had kept to herself. By doing that, however, might she have made herself look as though she didn't like the Creek people, or did not trust them?

She realized now that she must do things differently in order to gain their trust, especially to gain Swift Horse's admiration.

She glanced toward Abraham again, and saw how his head hung. He had fallen asleep, and she understood why. He was still surely trying to catch up on the rest he had lost while fleeing.

The thought of someone having actually held him imprisoned as a slave, and having actually killed his family, which was the true reason he had fled Florida, sickened Marsha. She had never believed in slavery and felt that all people should be free.

She admired Swift Horse for having taken a chance by allowing Abraham to stay among his people, when it was known, wide and far, that many Indians were now, by force, living on reservations. Those Indians, in a sense, were now no less than slaves themselves. She had to wonder if Swift Horse and his people lived in dread of this happening to them.

Her musings were interrupted when Swift Horse stood up, the shaman now walking away from him and past those who still sat. She gazed admirably at Swift Horse, again taken by his handsome appearance and his noble bearing.

In fringed buckskins and wearing a lone feather hanging from a lock of his long, raven-black hair, he stood tall over his people. With a straight back and lifted chin, he began talking to them about how the hunt had now been blessed and that the warriors would have a successful hunt for the white-tailed deer.

She caught him more than once look her way, then quickly look away again. When his eyes would touch her, it seemed as though he were trying to say something solely to her with them, and a sweet, strange tingle of sorts traveled along her flesh. She even blushed this last time he looked her way, smiling at him just before he looked into his crowd of people again.

Marsha realized that several of the women had noticed his attention to her, because they would look over their shoulders at her moments after Swift Horse had singled Marsha out with his deep, midnight-dark eyes.

Marsha could not help but blush at this new sort of attention from both this powerful, handsome chief and also the women who realized that their chief was surely infatuated with a woman of white skin, just the same as his sister felt for a man of the same skin color. But with no one voicing a negative opinion about Soft Wind planning to marry a white man, surely they would not say anything about a mere glance or two that their chief made toward the white man's sister.

"This council is now over," Swift Horse announced. "My brothers, the hunt *will* be good.

There will be much fresh meat for our families, and much meat to put away to eat during the longest, coldest days of winter, which are fast approaching us. Go home now to your families Enjoy this time with them, for soon you will be gone from them for as long as it takes to bring a good amount of deer meat into our village."

There were many grunts and nods of approval, and then everyone stood up. Some adults lingered and talked among others for a while as the children ran from them, laughing and squealing as they suddenly fell into a game of tag, or other games that Marsha saw as intriguing.

"Marsha, it's time to go," she heard her brother say, bringing her out of her reverie as she had found herself watching the children with a strange sort of longing that she had never felt before. All of her life she had loved children, but had never, even for a moment, thought of having her own. Now, as she watched the merriment all around her as the children laughed and played and ran and jumped, she did feel something inside her belly that she knew must be a longing to have a child of her own.

Suddenly her eyes went back to Swift Horse. A blush grew hot on her cheeks when she realized just where her thoughts had taken her, and then to whom.

"Marsha?" Edward James said as he reached down and gently took her by an elbow. "What on earth are you doing? What are you thinking so hard about? Come on. It's time to go home. The hunt council is over."

Marsha shook her head to clear her thoughts, then hurried to her feet and tried to avoid her brother's questioning stare. She realized just how oddly she had been behaving. She hardly recognized herself.

She walked with Edward James from the crowd, but could not help but take one last look over her shoulder at Swift Horse. Something within her grew warm and mellow when she saw his eyes dart quickly to her, their eyes locking and holding until someone said something to their chief, which drew his eyes away.

"I've never seen you act so strangely," Edward James said, gazing in wonder down at his sister, who was one head shorter than he. "Marsha, I saw you staring at Swift Horse. I'm sure others saw you, too. Are you infatuated with the man? Or is it just because he is a powerful chief?"

"Oh, Edward, I hope I didn't make a fool of myself," Marsha said, hurrying into the back door of their cabin, then turning to her brother when he stepped inside and closed the door behind them.

"Did I, Edward?" she asked, searching his eyes. "I couldn't help myself. I do find Swift Horse so fascinating."

"You mean handsome, don't you?" he said, chuckling as he went to the fireplace and lifted a log on the grate.

He brushed his hands on his pants and turned to Marsha. "I understand how you can be so caught up in wonder of that man," he said thickly. "I have been around a lot of Indians, but none like Swift Horse. As you have been witness to more than once, he is many things good— noble, kind, caring, and charitable. You have to know by now that he nor any of his people are anything like those who murdered our parents."

"Yes, I know, but . . ." Marsha said, feeling torn. She wanted to hate all redskins because of what had happened to her parents, yet she felt anything but hate for Swift Horse and his people, who had shown her nothing but kindness.

"Marsha, I have spoken with Swift Horse more than once about what happened to our parents and how it has affected you inside your heart," Edward James said, gently taking her hands in his. "Sis, he said that now that our family will soon be a part of his, he will try to help find those who murdered our parents."

"Truly?" Marsha said, her eyes wide with wonder. "He would do this?"

"Like I said, he is a kind man, and he hates all injustices, as you have witnessed by how he took in Abraham," Edward said, lowering his hands to his sides. "You know I'm right when I tell you that you should hold no ill feelings toward these Creek people. They would never condone what happened to our parents."

"Yes, I know," Marsha murmured.

She recalled how she had looked at Swift Horse just after she had been thinking about having children. She marveled even now at the thought, for to have children, you must first love the man who would have a role in bringing these children into the world. A woman must truly and especially trust and respect the man.

Strange how it could happen this quickly, but she knew that her feelings for Swift Horse were those that came with not only being infatuated with a man, but loving him.

"Sis?" Edward said, taking her hands once more. "You're gone from me again. What were you thinking about?"

Marsha felt the heat of a blush rush to her cheeks. "Don't you have somewhere to go?" she asked softly as she slid her hands from his. "Didn't you tell me that you were to meet with

Soft Wind after the council? Is she waiting for you?"

"Yes, and I truly must go," Edward said. "I just wanted to escort you home since you were behaving so oddly."

"I hope no one else noticed," Marsha said, then again saw Swift Horse in her mind's eye and how he had surely seen her infatuation with him those times their eyes had met and momentarily held.

"None know you as well as I, so they would not realize your behavior was different than usual—so, no, I doubt anyone noticed," Edward James said, reaching for a leather jacket that hung on a peg on the wall just inside the door. "I'll not be long, sis. I just so enjoy these special, stolen moments with my woman."

"I'll make a pot of chili for our supper," Marsha said, already walking toward their kitchen. She smiled over her shoulder at her brother. "If you wish, bring Soft Wind to sup with us."

"I doubt she would enjoy chili," he said, laughing softly. "It is too different from what she normally eats, don't you think?"

Marsha turned just as Edward James took hold of the latch on the door. "Will she cook when she marries you and moves into your . . .

our . . . cabin, or shall I?" she asked, locking her hands behind her.

"I would hope that you would teach each other your own different kitchen secrets," he said, winking at her.

"We shall," Marsha said, nodding. "Yes, we shall."

Edward James gave her another wink, then left.

Marsha sighed and went to the window. She saw how night had come quickly with its moon and stars. She thought about where her brother was going—to have a tryst with his beloved.

"Oh, how I wish it were me going to meet Swift Horse," she whispered to herself, her heart doing a strange sort of flip-flop when she saw Swift Horse step up to the great outdoor fire and begin talking with two of his warriors.

In the moonlight, and with his profile defined by the bright glow of the fire, he made her heart melt.

Chapter 7

It is, past escape,
Herself, now: the dream is done
And the shadow and she are one.
—Robert Browning

The hunt had only just begun a few days ago and already many Indians from other villages were at Marsha's brother's trading post, making trade. Even caravans of white traders, with their pack-horsemen to tend the animals, were there.

Marsha had watched the white traders coming into the village and noticed that the pack-horses were small, but Edward James had told her that they were capable of sustaining heavy loads and enduring great fatigue.

Her brother said that the load usually consisted of three bundles, weighing around sixty pounds. The whole pack was covered with a skin to keep off the rain, and poultry was carried in cages made of reeds strapped upon the horses' backs.

Marsha had seen that in addition to freshly

hunted venison, the Creek had also brought with them honey and beeswax, hickory nut oil, medicinal roots, and herbs to trade with.

Beautiful Creek baskets were among those things being brought in today, as well as pottery and finely dyed and decorated deerskins, and other articles that were sought by white settlers and travelers.

Marsha had quickly learned that an Indian could trade nine ears of corn in return for a single used Cherokee stroud blanket. This was a tremendous bargain for the Creeks, for the price of a new blanket was approximately eight dressed deerskins.

Since so many had arrived at Swift Horse's village to trade, Marsha had no choice but to help her brother in the store. She had learned quickly enough to give her brother the assistance he needed at a time when, if he didn't have help, he would lose much money.

She hurried through the motions of what was required of her to get her through this day, wishing to be back in the privacy of their home, away from those who were not of this village.

She couldn't feel comfortable in the crowded store. Those who had killed her parents could be among the traders, pretending to be friendly, whereas in truth, they would as soon kill her brother and her as look at them.

She had hoped that Swift Horse would come today for trade, for she had thought he would be among his warriors on the hunt. But her brother had said that others were hunting, while he remained in the village to be sure no one came into their fold who were not supposed to be there. She hadn't seen him at all, but knew that he must be keeping a close watch from his cabin as people came and went to trade.

She tried to focus her thoughts on what she was supposed to be doing now, being careful that she was right in what she gave those who came with their beautiful pelts for trade. She constantly went through it in her head—cloth was measured by the yard, or was traded in pre-cut pieces.

Beads were sold by the strand, and vermilion was measured by the amount that covered the tip of a knife.

The skin of a mature buck usually weighed about two pounds, whereas dressed skins from younger bucks and does might weigh only one pound. A dressed skin that weighed one pound was called a chalk, and larger skins, depending on weight, were worth two or three chalks.

Raw skins weighed three pounds, and were

bought by tally, reflecting their lower value. She was stunned to know that white traders lopped the snouts, ears, horns and hooves off the deer-skins. This was a tactic that offended the Indians' sensibilities in addition to reducing the weight of the skin, but traders claimed that good, well-dressed and trimmed skins reduced the weight of carriage, and better preserved the hides.

She had been surprised the first time she dis-covered a practice at her brother's trading post—that sometimes tallies were kept there by the use of vertical and diagonal lines so that the Creek customers that frequented his trading post could clearly see their credits and debits.

For one pound of half-dressed leather, a Creek could buy twenty strands of common beads, forty bullets, one dozen pea buttons, a small knife, ten to twelve flints, one half pint of gunpowder, about one yard of ribbon, one pair of scissors, or one ounce of vermilion. A duffel blanket, at eight pounds of leather, and trade guns, at sixteen pounds of leather or more, were among the most expensive goods.

Saddles, priced from thirty to sixty pounds of leather, were seldom purchased. More often, they were acquired as presents or given as re-wards for service. Horse bridles cost four pounds of leather. Indians paid from six to ten pounds of leather for horse blankets called *housing*, depending on quality.

Fabric prices ranged from one pound of leather for three or four yards of caddis to eight pounds of leather for two yards of heavier wool cloth. The prices of ready-to-wear shirts ranged from three pounds of leather for a plain white shirt to eight pounds of leather for a fine-checked or ruffled shirt.

Her back aching, her head pounding from the constant work and attention to what needed to be done, Marsha stepped back from the counter and stretched her arms overhead, then kneaded the small of her back as she slowly looked around her. She had been too busy earlier to look carefully at who was there, except for those she had tended to at the counter. But now she saw just how many diverse people there were and was amazed at how her brother seemed to know so many of them as he went from one to the other, talking business.

Suddenly her throat constricted when she saw the renegade among those who stood across the room from her brother, amidst the crowd of Indians, yet not actually talking with any of them. Instead, he was staring at her with a sort of loathing that made chills ride her spine.

"Lord, it *is* him," Marsha whispered to

herself, not so surprised when this discovery made her tremble. How could she ever forget how he had so heartlessly murdered her parents, and how he had seemed to single her out for a moment before he rode off, soon lost amidst dust that was created by his and his friends' horses?

Ignoring those who were standing in line waiting for her to assist them, she searched for her brother. When she found him, she saw that he was busy talking with several Creek warriors now, making trade, but she had no choice but to interrupt him.

He had to know. He had to stop the renegade. He must tie him up and then take him to the fort, for arresting.

She rushed from behind the counter and went to her brother. "Edward," she said, trying to get his attention. "Edward James, I'm sorry to interrupt, but I've something to tell you. It's ... it's ..."

He turned to her with a glower that was new to her, but she understood why. He might lose money because of her interference. But she had to tell him.

"Edward James, the one-eyed man—"

"Sis," he said, taking her gently by the arm and ushering her a few inches away from those who still stood awaiting his decision about what their pelts were worth.

"I'm in the middle of something," Edward James said. "Give me a chance to finish and then—"

"Edward James!" Marsha said, truly stunned by his being this inattentive to her, especially when he had surely heard her start to say something about the one-eyed man.

She gave him a stare of wonder, then jerked herself free and ran from the cabin, sobbing.

When she was outside, with the noise of the trading post behind her, she stopped and wiped at her eyes, wondering what she was to do.

He had surely recognized her. Would he come for her and finish what he had not been able to do on the day of the ambush?

"Swift Horse!" she whispered to herself, looking quickly toward his cabin. Her heart warmed at the sight of him as he stood at his door. "Yes, I shall seek his help," she whispered to herself, and broke into a run toward him.

Swift Horse was suddenly aware of Marsha coming toward him, a frantic sort of look in her eyes, and could only conclude that her brother must be having some trouble inside his store.

He hurried toward her and met her halfway to see what was troubling her. When she stopped before him, she could hardly catch her breath, her eyes wild as she gazed up at him.

"What has happened?" he asked, taking her gently by her shoulders. "You are upset. Why? Is it something that happened at your brother's store?"

Again she breathed hard, sucked in deep gulps of air, then was finally able to talk. "No, it is not what has happened there—" she rushed out, her eyes pleading into his. "Swift Horse, you've got to help me. The man who murdered my parents is at my brother's store. The one-eyed man. He's there! He must be taken into custody. He must be made to pay for what he did!"

When Swift Horse was aware of her distress and heard her describe someone who was one-eyed, he could only conclude that she had mistaken his friend, for he had seen One Eye go into the store only a short while ago, a stack of pelts in his arms for trade.

"Do not be in such distress, for the man you saw is my friend, whose name is One Eye," Swift Horse said softly. "I saw him arrive a short while ago. He is there to make trade with your brother."

"You are mistaken," Marsha said, stunned that he was taking this news this easily when he had been told by her brother how their parents had died on their way from Georgia to his village. "The man in there is the one who killed my parents. I have no doubt that it is he."

"Did you see more than one one-eyed man in the store?" Swift Horse asked gently.

"No," Marsha said, almost knowing what his next words would be, and disappointed that he was not taking her seriously.

"Then the one-eyed man is definitely my friend, for I saw him go there," Swift Horse reiterated, lowering his hands from her shoulders.

"Then it is your friend who I saw murder my parents, because I shall never forget him! Never!" Marsha cried.

Again taking her gently by the shoulders, Swift Horse leaned closer down into her face. "Marsha, I know my friend well," he said thickly. "We have been friends since we were young braves learning the ways of warriors. He is not a murderer. He is a man of heart and a warrior praised for his bravery. I was with him when he was injured by a bear he downed to save *me*. That is why his one eye is missing. He is admired by all for his prowess, kindness, and intelligence."

Marsha could not be dissuaded. She reached up and removed his hands from her arms and started slowly backing away from him. "I know what I know," she said tightly. "I know that he was among those who killed not only my parents, but several of the soldiers who were escorting us from Georgia to Kentucky. Surely there can't be two men with the same empty socket and same livid white scar that runs down from where the eye had once been."

Swift Horse saw her determination. He had to prove her wrong. He took her gently by an elbow and began ushering her back toward the trading post. "I will take you and introduce you to One Eye," he said, stunned when she yanked herself away from him and glared at him, then ran from him.

Marsha was devastated that Swift Horse wouldn't believe her. There she was, in mortal danger, with the very man who killed her parents and who had looked at her with such hate, at the store, and still Swift Horse wouldn't believe her.

She hurried back toward the store, alone. Her brother had been too involved in trading earlier to listen to her, and had actually told her not to interfere. But now that no longer mattered. He had to listen to her. She had to make him understand that the man he hated with every fiber of his being was there—so close to them both that he could murder them.

Pushing her way through the crowd, very aware that people were lined up from the door to the counter where she should be helping her brother, Marsha ignored them and went to her brother and took him by an arm and spoke his name.

When he turned and glared at her again, obviously still wanting her to stop interfering, she grabbed him by an arm and half dragged him away from those with whom he was talking trade. She took him to a far corner, then turned him to face her.

"You must listen to me, Edward James," she said, placing her fists on her hips. "And *look.*"

She nodded toward the one-eyed man who was still there but this time talking with others, seemingly for the moment forgetting about her. "There he is, Edward James," she said, her voice trembling as she pointed at him. "Do you see him now? He's the one I described to you. He's the one, Edward James. He killed our parents."

Edward scanned the crowd, then stopped when he saw who she was referring to.

He turned to her, a renewed irritated look in his eyes. "You are mistaken," he said. "This man is Swift Horse's best friend, a man who is chief of his Wolf Clan. I have talked often with One Eye. We have also smoked from the same pipe, as friends. One Eye is a rich Creek chief. Why would he have a need to ambush and kill people?"

Marsha stepped closer and spoke into her brother's face. "An evil man needs no true reason to kill," she said, her eyes dancing angrily into his. "It is not so much for money. It is for the sheer pleasure—the excitement of the kill."

"Sis, if you can't do anything but stir up trouble, I'd rather you stay in the living quarters from now on," Edward James said. He pointed toward the door that led there. "Go now. Forget your foolish notion of who you think this man is."

Swift Horse came into the cabin and went to Marsha and Edward James.

"I apologize for my sister," Edward James said, seeing by Swift Horse's demeanor that he knew of Marsha's accusations. "Marsha is mistaken. Marsha, tell him that you're mistaken," Edward James said, turning pleading eyes to her.

Finding this so unbelievable, that both her brother and Swift Horse could be so blind and unreasonable, Marsha gave them each an angry stare, then spun around and stamped away. Just as she reached the door that led into the living quarters, she took a look over her shoulder.

Her knees weakened and she felt as though she might vomit when she found One Eye glaring at her with the same contemptuous look that he had given her on the day of the massacre.

Breathless, almost fainting, she hurried into the living quarters and slammed the door and leaned against it. She felt trapped. She must go for help. Someone had to believe her. One Eye must be taken into custody, or she was a woman staring death in the face. And so was her precious brother.

She grabbed a cloak, swung it around her shoulders and tied it, then fled through the back door. She mounted her white mare, White Cloud, and rode away through the forest toward Fort Hill. Surely those in authority there would believe her.

Oh, Lord, she thought to herself. They must believe her, or she didn't have that much longer on this earth. She knew that One Eye would kill her.

She thought about Swift Horse. How could he be this deceived by such a man as One Eye?

Chapter 8

The Devil had he fidelity,
Would be the finest friend—
Because he has ability,
But Devils cannot mend.
> —Emily Dickinson

Determined to get One-Eye behind bars, Marsha rode hard on her horse. Her golden hair was flying in the wind behind her, and the skirt of her dress had blown up, fluttering now past her knees. The coolness of the autumn day's breeze caused her cheeks to burn as she continued on her way.

She snapped the reins against the rump of her steed, sending her white mare into an even harder gallop. "Giddyup, White Cloud!" she shouted. "We can't let the man go into hiding again! The nerve of him! How could he mingle with everyone as though he is innocent of all wrongdoing?"

She smiled almost victoriously when she thought of how he had behaved when he first caught her looking at him across the room at the store. A keen knowing, intermingled with fear, flashed in his eyes. At that moment he knew that he had been caught, yet . . .

"Yet then he just glared at me," she cried. "He didn't flee."

She now knew why. He felt confident enough in depending on both Swift Horse and her brother to speak in his behalf.

Oddly enough, the very man who had taken her brother's parents away was a *friend* of her brother's, who surely traded at the store many times, surely even with blood having been fresh on his hands only moments before he arrived.

"You'll pay," she sobbed. "Damn you, you one-eyed beast, I will make you pay if no one else will!"

She rode free of the forest and led her steed across a flat stretch of land. She knew that the soldiers at Fort Hill worked in unison with all of the surrounding villages of Indians.

The fort kept the Indians "in line," even though they knew Swift Horse to be a man of peace. But again, there were those Indians who weren't peace-loving, who needed to be watched. If a skirmish broke out between Indians and the white people, she had to believe that the Indians would be the victors, for there were far more of them in this area than settlers or soldiers.

However, the Indians were surely smart enough to know that although there were only a few soldiers at Fort Hill now, many more soldiers could arrive from other forts if summoned. Together they could stop an Indian rebellion in no time flat.

She hoped that everyone continued to live together in peace, and her brother was there to help it along, for he was a friend to everyone, both white and red-skinned.

"Maybe that's why he won't allow himself to believe what I told him," she whispered to herself.

Riding onward, Marsha was aware of something in the air that made her insides tighten.

She smelled smoke. The wind seemed to be carrying it from the direction of the fort. Her blood chilled at the thought of Indians having gone there, and set it afire. Had some of them decided to try to run the soldiers off land that had at one time belonged solely to the red man?

If so, why now? What would prompt it?

It was obvious that the hunt was good this season. She had seen the proof of this at her brother's trading post. Perhaps some had not been as lucky, and decided to take it out on those who lived at the fort.

Marsha traveled onward, and soon found herself meeting clouds and bursts of smoke. She saw animals running scared in the opposite direction—deer racing past her, their eyes wild with fear, as well as tiny forest animals.

She knew that she should stop and turn back, but if the fort had been attacked and those who survived needed help, perhaps she could assist in some small way until more help came.

But she soon found herself riding into a thicker, billowing smoke that caused her eyes to burn and her throat to sting. She knew that she had no choice now but to turn back. The smoke attested to a big fire up ahead. She had to make a fast retreat or meet it head-on and then she wouldn't have a chance of escaping it.

Just as she drew a tight rein to stop and wheel her steed around to go back in the direction she had just come, White Cloud whinnied and bucked, but Marsha managed to hold on and wasn't thrown.

"White Cloud, come on!" she cried, sinking her heels into the mare's flanks, urging it onward. "Please get me out of here!"

She soon discovered, after riding only a few feet, that the fire had not only been ahead of her.

She saw it now in a huge, wide circle all around her, advancing on her, the smoke now so thick she felt as though her throat was on fire.

"Lord!" she cried, only now recalling how the Creek had talked during the hunt council about how some were going to use fire for their hunt today; how it was used to frighten deer so much they went insane with the need to flee, only then to find themselves at the mercy of the Creek hunters.

"Hunters!" she whispered, a cold dread washing through her to think that she might be amidst a firing range if the hunters were standing just beyond the flames, waiting to shoot at anything that moved, thinking it was deer.

Thus far, she had seen only a few, but she knew that the Creek knew this land and would understand how many deer to expect to flee the fire.

Now truly feeling trapped, White Cloud nervously pawing at the ground, her nostrils flaring, seemingly frozen by fear, Marsha dismounted. "Is anyone near?" she screamed, as the fire slowly advanced in the circle all around her, burning everything in its path.

She wasn't sure which way she should go. Fire and smoke were everywhere!

"Please!" she cried as she stumbled away from her horse, tears streaming from her eyes. "Someone come and help me!" Then she stopped dead in her tracks. She saw a little fawn trapped, too, amidst the flames.

The smoke choking her, Marsha made her way toward the fawn that now lay on the ground, its eyes closed, perhaps dead! But Marsha couldn't leave it there. Perhaps it was still alive, even if only barely. She must save it!

The smoke was choking Marsha. Her eyes were burning so badly now she could hardly see one inch ahead of her, but she finally reached the tiny animal. She leaned down over it and saw that one of its legs was broken.

Marsha was very aware of the heat. It penetrated the soles of her shoes.

Trembling now, truly afraid that she wasn't going to make it to safety, nor be able to save the tiny creature or her beloved horse, she still bent low and swept the fawn into her arms.

Holding it close to her chest, she struggled to find a way through the smoke and the flames, moving around in a circle as she searched, staggering now, coughing.

The flames were closing in, and she couldn't find an opening for her escape.

She saw her life flashing before her eyes before dropping the fawn and blacking out, falling limply toward the ground.

Chapter 9

He is made one with Nature: there is heard
His voice in all her music, from the moan
Of thunder, to the song of night's sweet bird.
— Percy Bysshe Shelley

Having seen the smoke, Alan Burton, whom so many called Cowkeeper, rode hard toward it on his black stallion. Anger swelled inside him because he knew why things were afire today, yet had to see it for himself. He especially had to see how much land it was consuming and just how close it might get to his ranch, where his cows were innocently grazing on tall, green grass.

He found it hard to believe that the Creek were using this method to hunt, when from all of his observations, there were plenty of deer to just go out and shoot!

"But, no," he cried to the heavens. "They had to set good land afire!" He was so angry he could hardly contain it.

The fires were eating up grazing grasses, and risked killing tiny, innocent forest animals that would get caught amidst the flames.

"The fools!" he shouted, raising a fist above his head and swinging it.

He coughed when he found himself engulfed in a thicker, rolling smoke. He covered his mouth with a hand and blinked his eyes to clear them of the sting, yet he rode onward.

His eyes narrowed angrily when he finally saw the flames up ahead that were sending off the ungodly smoke that had reached as far as his ranch. He urged his horse forward to see just how far the flames were reaching, coughing and choking the farther he rode.

Realizing that he had gone his limit, yet close enough now to see the huge circle of fire, he drew a tight rein and patted his horse on the neck. He could feel the fear in his horse, and as it yanked on the reins and looked back at him, he saw it in the wildness of its eyes.

"It's okay, boy," Alan reassured his stallion.

He started to wheel his horse around to head back for home, but stopped, swallowed hard, and wiped at his eyes to see if he was imagining things or if he had seen a woman lying amidst the flames. He looked again through his stinging eyes. His heart skipped a beat when he realized that what he had seen was real enough. A woman lay within the circle of fire, the fire slowly inching its way toward her.

"Lord amighty!" he cried as he leaped from his horse. His hands trembled as he grabbed a blanket from his saddlebag.

He looked anxiously around him for the creek that he knew should be there but was momentarily hidden behind the smoke. The smoke separated and there it was.

Water!

He ran to the creek and fell to his knees, dunking the blanket into the water and soaking it thoroughly. Then he stood up, and as he ran back in the direction of the flames, he threw the blanket over himself, leaving enough of his face exposed in order for him to see where he was going.

Gathering his courage, he swallowed hard, then bravely ran through the fire, feeling the heat even through the wetness of the blanket and the soles of his boots.

He knelt down beside the woman. He hoped that she was still alive, but he didn't have the time to check for a pulse. The important thing was to get her to safety.

His eyes darted over to the tiny creature that lay beside the woman. He knew that it might already be dead because of smoke inhalation, but if Alan succeeded at getting the woman freed of this damnable fire and smoke, he would try to rescue the fawn, as well.

He swept Marsha into his arms, hating to feel just how limp she was. Hopefully he was in time and wouldn't die while trying to save her.

Holding the blanket over them both now, he sucked in a wild breath, then held it as he ducked low over Marsha and ran again through the fire. He didn't stop until he had Marsha safely away from the flames and stretched out beside the creek.

The blanket resting around his shoulders, Alan placed trembling fingers to Marsha's throat and sighed with relief when he did feel a pulse. He looked toward the flames again. He knew what he must do.

He wetted down the blanket again, swept it over him, and soon had the fawn back beside Marsha. Alan examined the fawn's neck and was relieved when he felt a strong pulse. Then he tossed the blanket aside and concentrated on the woman.

He cupped his hands together, sank them into the creek, and brought out as much water in them as he could. He slowly drizzled the water over Marsha's face in hopes of reviving her.

When she still didn't awaken, he washed her face clean of as much ash as he could, then sprinkled water across her lips, all the while gazing upon her and seeing her loveliness through the ash.

Now that her face was cleared enough, he recognized her. He had seen her at the back of the trading post, hanging clothes. He had heard about a sister having come to live with the storekeeper.

Because of a recent confrontation with Edward James Eveland, he knew that he wasn't welcome at the trading post for a while. Looking from a distance was all that he could do at that time. Hopefully things would change now that he had rescued the woman.

He smiled slyly at that thought. Yes! A reward would be offered, and he would refuse it. Just having the opportunity to go to the trading post again, to make trade and to see the woman again, would be reward enough.

As he continued bathing her face, hoping that she would soon awaken, Alan thought about how lonely he had been since the death of his wife. This woman could be the answer to that loneliness. Surely she would be grateful enough to him to allow him to court her.

Ah, what a beautiful bed partner she would

make. Now that a portion of the ash was removed from her face, Alan winced when he saw
the slight burns on one cheek.

Suddenly his insides tightened when he saw
her eyelashes fluttering as she slowly awakened.

She coughed throatily, then gazed up at Alan.
Marsha smiled at the man and attempted to say,
"Thank you," through her parched throat, then
blacked out again.

Glad that he had saved both the woman and
the fawn, and that she had awakened long
enough to see that he was the one who did it,
Alan carried Marsha to his horse and laid her beside it. He went back for the fawn and took it and
slid it inside his saddlebag, leaving its face exposed, its eyes now wide and watching. Then
Alan lifted Marsha onto his lap on his horse, po-
sitioning her so that her head rested against his
chest.

Smiling triumphantly, Alan knew this good
deed would most certainly get him on the good
side of her brother. He needed Edward James's
support against Swift Horse, to get his way
about things. He slapped his reins and rode
away from the flames and smoke, then went cold
inside when Swift Horse was suddenly there,
blocking his way.

"Hand the woman over to me," Swift Horse

said, his dark eyes glaring at Alan. "I saw her leave her home and made chase but lost track of her until moments ago when I saw her amidst the fire."

Alan hesitated, then said, "Absolutely not," his jaw tight. "I saved her. I'll take her home to her brother."

Swift Horse edged his steed closer to Alan's. "Cowkeeper, you do not seem to understand," he said, with an edge to his voice. "I saw her when you saw her. You just reached her before I had the chance to. Hand the woman over to my care now, or regret it later. I will take her to her brother."

Marsha awakened through their argument. She saw Swift Horse demanding that she be handed over to him. She had heard Swift Horse call the man Cowkeeper and then realized the company she was in. Everyone despised this man, including her brother.

She gazed up at Alan and shifted her weight in his arms. He felt her movement and looked quickly down at her.

"I would rather be returned home by Swift Horse," she said through her parched throat. "Please be so kind as to give me over to him."

Disgruntled, Alan saw that he had no choice.

He gently placed her in Swift Horse's arms, and the chief positioned her on his lap.

"I . . . also . . . want the fawn," she said. She looked around her, deeply saddened to believe that White Cloud had more than likely perished in the fire.

She heard Alan grumble something to himself as he reached inside his saddlebag and slid the fawn free. Marsha reached her arms out for the tiny thing. Alan's eyes met Marsha's for a moment, then he placed the animal in her arms.

Alan glared at Swift Horse. He felt cheated. He would surely not reap any rewards for having saved the beautiful lady, but he would still find a way to use what he had done in his favor.

He wheeled his horse around and rode toward his home. After traveling a short distance, he spied a beautiful white horse standing at the creek, drinking freely of it.

He looked in the direction of where he had last seen the woman being taken away by Swift Horse, and smiled. This steed must be hers! He rode up to it and grabbed its reins and again headed for home.

Having something of the woman's was certainly in his favor! Perhaps it could be used to lure her to his home. But, no! *He* would take it *to* her!

He smiled as he rode onward, glad to leave the flames and smoke behind.

Chapter 10

I fear thy kisses, gentle maiden,
Thou needest not fear mine;
My spirit is too deeply laden
Even to burthen thine.
—Percy Bysshe Shelley

Swift Horse rode toward the trading post just as Edward James stepped onto the front porch with a warrior from a neighboring village.

Edward James's arm was around the warrior's shoulder, talking and laughing—until Edward James saw whom Swift Horse was carrying on his steed.

"Marsha!" he gasped, racing down the steps to meet Swift Horse. "Lord, what happened?" Edward James asked as he came up next to Swift Horse's mount. He reached his arms up for his sister just as she opened her eyes and gazed down at him through the ash that still lay heavy on her lashes.

"Edward James . . ." she said through her parched throat. "I did an unwise thing, I—"

"Don't talk," Edward James said as Swift Horse placed her into her brother's arms. "Your throat. I can tell . . ."

"It was the smoke," Swift Horse said, dismounting. "She collapsed amidst the circle of flame that was set by my warriors." Swift Horse then told Edward James about having found Marsha with the cowkeeper and how he had demanded her to be given to him.

"Why was she with him?" Edward James asked.

"Edward James, it was . . . it was . . . because of the one-eyed man that I did this," Marsha managed to say before her throat became too raw to say anything else.

"You did it because of *what*?" Edward James said, gazing incredulously into her eyes. "Marsha . . ."

"She came to me for help when she saw One Eye at your store, and thinking it was the one-eyed man who killed your parents, sought my help—" Swift Horse began, but was interrupted when Marsha broke in.

"The man I saw at the store *was* the man I saw the day my parents died," Marsha managed to say through the burning of her throat. "You wouldn't listen, so I . . ." But her throat being so parched and achy, she couldn't continue on.

She hung her head, for she knew that neither man believed her. Would they ever?

"The man you call One Eye *is* the man who—" Marsha tried to say, finding it hard to give in to the pain until she made these two understand, but her throat gave way, the pain so intense she even found it hard to swallow now. She had inhaled much smoke, and her lungs ached.

She managed to direct a soft thank you at Swift Horse for having come for her—for she would have hated being taken to the cowkeeper's home—before drifting off to sleep, her body as well as her lungs too traumatized by the fire to stay awake.

"Edward James, I know no more than what I have told you," Swift Horse said tightly. "I went after your sister when she left the village, but I did not find her soon enough—yet had I been much longer, I would not want to think about the result."

He gazed toward the smoke in the distance, then at Edward James, who still stood there, his eyes transfixed on his sister. "Everyone was warned about the fires being set today," he said with regret in his voice. "Since your sister has not been in the area long enough to understand the true dangers, she did not take it into consideration when she rode from the safety of the village."

"But why on earth did she leave?" Edward James said, more to himself than to Swift Horse as he turned and walked up the steps, leaving Swift Horse standing beside his horse, watching until Edward James went inside the trading post.

"The fawn," Abraham said suddenly behind Swift Horse, causing Swift Horse to turn with a start, then smile as he saw his friend taking the tiny animal from his travel bag at the side of his steed.

Swift Horse went to Abraham, who held the tiny animal gingerly in his arms, his dark eyes studying the one limp leg.

"It is broken," Abraham said. He looked quickly up at Swift Horse. "I can make it well."

Abraham smiled almost shyly at Swift Horse. "I love animals, large and small, but I have never owned one," he said softly. "But I knows tiny animals well from rescuing those that got lost in the swamps of Florida land. I always took them home and doctored them, then returned them to the wild. I can do the same for this tiny animal. May I?"

"Yes, it is yours to see to, if you wish to," Swift Horse said, placing a gentle hand on his friend's shoulder. "But it would not be wise to send it back into the forest just yet, for its mother might have become a part of the hunt."

"The lady?" Abraham asked, his eyes filled with a sudden concern. "What happened to the lady?"

"All I know is that she got trapped within the circle of flames that had been set for my warriors' hunt," Swift Horse said thickly. "It is good that that circle was far and wide, for that is the only reason the woman made it out of this alive."

"Why did she go there?" Abraham asked, the curiosity still in his wide, dark eyes. "She has a home and a brother. Why would she want to flee them?"

"She has her reasons, and soon her brother will know them," Swift Horse said, turning and gazing at the trading post. "I hope to know them, too."

"I wish her well," Abraham said, swallowing hard.

"I do, as well, for if she does not survive this, I will feel responsible," Swift Horse said, sighing heavily.

"But you did not send her into the fire," Abraham reasoned out. "So you should not feel responsible."

"I feel responsible for her not being made to

understand the dangers of our people's hunts,"
Swift Horse said, again sighing.

"She will survive this," Abraham reassured.
"Just you wait and see. Then you can teach her as
you have taught everyone else of this village
what is dangerous and what is not." Abraham
stepped closer to Swift Horse and placed a hand
on his shoulder. "You are a wise man," he said
seriously. "You are a kind-hearted, gentle, wise
man."

"Thank you," Swift Horse said, smiling at
Abraham. He then reached out and stroked the
fawn's back as the tiny animal gazed trustingly
back at him. "Take the animal," he said. "It has
trust in its eyes and heart for you."

"It will be the first thing that I have been free
to love," Abraham said, tears filling his eyes. He
gave Swift Horse a humble look. "Again, thank
you."

Swift Horse only nodded and then watched
Abraham take the fawn away to his cabin. He
looked over his shoulder again at the trading
post, his thoughts now again filled with Marsha.
Had he not come along and stopped the cowkeeper from taking her, perhaps no one would
have ever seen her again.

He knew how scheming a man Alan Burton
was, and being now without a wife, who was to

say what his plans had been for Marsha? Even thinking of the possibility of that man having taken her to his home with plans of keeping her made a flash of heated hate rush through him. He would make certain that the cowkeeper wouldn't come close to Marsha again, and he would also do what he could to make her well.

He would send Bright Moon to Marsha. Bright Moon would do his magic, and the beautiful woman Swift Horse now knew that he loved would soon be well again.

His heart warmed as he thought of that moment when she had said thank you through her parched throat and smiled so sweetly at him. The thing that he must do was try to make this up to her by finding the one-eyed man who was truly guilty and at the same time prove that his friend was innocent of such crimes!

Chapter 11

Up, to thy wonted work! come, trace
The epitaph of glory fled;
For now the Earth has changed its face,
A frown is on the Heaven's brow.
—Percy Bysshe Shelley

One Eye had been ready to leave the village when he saw Marsha being brought home in Swift Horse's arms.

"I must find a way to silence her forever, but cast the guilt elsewhere," he whispered to himself, glowering as he now watched Swift Horse hurry to his shaman's cabin. If One Eye had his way, he would kill the shaman so that he could not help the woman.

A sudden thought came to him that made him grin. He shifted himself in his saddle and rode away from the village, smiling even more broadly.

Yes, he had a plan. It would surely work!

He knew how much the cowkeeper was hated by Swift Horse and his people, and even

Edward James Eveland, the village storekeeper. The cowkeeper was presently without a wife. Perhaps the cowkeeper could be the person the woman's brother, as well as Swift Horse, would suspect, if Marsha came up missing. They would think that Alan Burton had taken her!

One Eye would kill Marsha and then plant her dead body in the cowkeeper's house after he killed Alan Burton.

One Eye would make it appear as though the cowkeeper and Marsha had struggled and that she had been able to stab the cowkeeper with his knife after he had inflicted a deadly wound on her. They would be found dead, together, at the cowkeeper's house.

Smiling wickedly, One Eye rode from the village. He knew to avoid the area where the hunt was in progress.

While the woman lived, she was too much of a threat to One Eye's existence, for although no one believed her, she knew that it was he who had killed her parents, and it was apparent that she would stop at nothing to prove his guilt!

He laughed throatily, thinking how stupid Swift Horse was to believe that his one-eyed friend, the chief of the Wolf Clan of Creek, could never do anything as evil as the ambushes and murders that he had done.

One Eye even had the blood of Swift Horse's very own parents on his hands! He killed for the fun of it, not for what he gained from it otherwise.

Chapter 12

O! let me have thee whole,—all—all—
be mine!
That shape, that fairness. . . .
—John Keats

"Sis!" Edward James said as she meandered into his store several days later.

He rushed to her as she stopped and teetered somewhat, grabbing for her and holding her steady. "Sis, I told you not to leave your bed today," he said thickly. "I can do whatever needs to be done."

"I don't think I'm ready to eat any of your cooking, Edward James," Marsha said, giggling. She smiled up at him from her shorter height. "Big brother, I am much, much better today. Can't you see that? I've come to the store for some flour. I plan to make bread."

"No, you don't," Edward James said, taking her by an arm and trying to turn her back in the direction of their home, but she stayed firm. "If you won't stay in bed, at least sit by the fire and crochet or read. Truly, sis. I know how to cook. Who do you think cooked for me before you came?"

She gave him a look he understood well. She believed that Soft Wind had been cooking for him . . . and probably many more things.

"Well, yes, Soft Wind did bring me supper now and then," Edward said, absently running his fingers through his thick rusty-red hair. "But you have to know that wasn't immediately after I arrived here. I didn't know her yet."

"I'm sure Swift Horse made certain the women of the village kept you in nourishing food," Marsha said, then winced and reached her hand to her cheek, where her burn still pained her despite Bright Moon's medicine.

"See there?" Edward James said, gently taking her by an arm. "You are still in pain. I'm going to take you back to the living quarters. I insist you lie down, at least for the rest of the morning. And then, if you must, prepare something simple for supper."

"Perhaps you are right," Marsha said, taking a step toward the door that led into their home, then stopped with a start and spun around when the front door of the store opened and then slammed closed. Her insides tightened when she saw Alan Burton standing there, the wide grin on his whiskered face revealing where one tooth was missing.

Edward James turned and his hands curved into tight fists when he saw that the cowkeeper had actually come into the trading post when he knew that he wasn't welcome. He had become a thorn in everyone's side in the area. Knowing just how much trouble he caused, time and again, for Swift Horse and his people, Edward James walked angrily toward the man.

Alan ignored Edward James. "Good mornin' to you, ma'am," he said, lifting his wide-brimmed hat from his head and going through the motions of a mock bow.

He straightened his back, his eyes still on Marsha, and still very openly ignoring Edward James's presence. "Ma'am, I've come to pay my respects," he said thickly. "It pleases me to see how well you are after the traumatic experience that you had the other day. It is good to see you up and out of bed and doing so well."

His smile waned when he gazed at the slight burn on her right cheek. He nodded toward it. "I regret not being able to save you from that one burn," he said. "But I feel that you are lucky if that is all that came from your moments in that circle of fire."

He glared suddenly at Edward James, who stepped up in front of him, blocking his view of Marsha. "Step aside, storekeeper," he said, placing a hand on Edward James's shoulder and giving him a half shove. "I've come to pay my respects to your lovely sister. If you recall, it was I who saved her from that hellish fire that the Injuns set. They know the dangers. Not only does it destroy good vegetation and kill small animals, this time it almost killed your sister."

"Give me one more shove and you'll get a whipping you'll never forget," Edward James said, grabbing Alan's wrist and moving it away from him, then releasing it. He leaned into the man's face. "And you'd best forget your obvious intentions toward my sister. You aren't good enough to even shine her shoes, so turn around and get outta here or be sorry for ignoring my warnings."

"I'd be careful who you're giving warnings to," Alan said, yet took a step away from Edward James, an uneasiness in his beady gray eyes.

"Get this, Cowkeeper," Edward James said, stepping closer to the man. "I'm giving you another warning, and let me see what you are going to do about it. Scat. I don't want the likes of you at my trading post. Turn around and go back to where you came from, and while you're at it, take my warnings about my sister with you. Forget you ever saw her. Do you hear?"

"Just like I should've ignored her the other day as though I didn't see her?" Alan said, laughing throatily. "Had I not came along, she'd have died. You're an ungrateful sort, but I didn't expect much more than that from you. You've sided with the Injuns in the area. You might as well exchange blood with them and be one of 'em, yourself."

"If you came for a thank you for what you did, all right, I'll tell you that I am much obliged that you saved my sister," Edward James said, sliding his hands into his front breeches pockets, something Marsha knew that her brother did when he was frustrated about something. She knew that he would have rather had his eyeteeth pulled than thank this man for anything.

"Now that's more like it," Alan said, smiling victoriously as he took a step to the right, which again gave him a full view of Marsha. "Ma'am, I'd appreciate it if you'd accept my invitation to sit and talk with me someday soon. My wife died not all that long ago. I've been mighty starved for female companionship."

Marsha's eyes widened in disbelief, changing to horror when she realized why this man was there. He didn't just want their thanks for having saved her. He was actually making advances toward her.

She looked quickly at Edward James, awaiting his explosion, but she saw that although his eyes were lit with fire, he kept his temper under control. But she didn't know for how much longer.

"Cowkeeper, I think you'd best consider not carrying this role of 'hero' you're playing much farther," Edward James said between his clenched teeth. "Like I said, I am much obliged for you having saved my sister, but that does not give you an iota of a claim on her. In other words, Cowkeeper, neither she nor I owe you anything."

He took a step closer to Alan again. "And had you not happened along just when you did, someone else was there to rescue her," he said tightly. "Swift Horse was only a few feet away. Had you not been there, Swift Horse would've saved Marsha."

"It does not erase the fact that I *did* save her, not Swift Horse," Alan said bitterly. "And I have come to get my dues. All I want is some time with your sister, to talk, nothin' more. Now is that askin' too much for what I did?"

Marsha stepped up beside Edward James. She placed a gentle hand on his arm. "Edward James, Alan did save me," she murmured. "I do owe him something."

"Marsha!" Edward James gasped, paling. "What are you saying?"

She turned and faced the cowkeeper, feeling sick inside at the look of hope on his face and in his anxious eyes. He was taking what she was about to do—was about to say—in the wrong way. He was actually feeling hopeful.

"Sir, I am grateful for what you did for me," she said softly. "But I must decline your offer. My brother is a good judge of character. Yes, I am grateful, but that is as far as any of this will go."

"Why, you bi—" he began, but stopped short. Edward James had yanked his fists from his pockets, ready to defend his sister if she was wronged in any way.

"I should take your horse home with me and forget I rescued it for you," Alan said bitterly.

"White Cloud?" Marsha gasped, her eyes widening. "You found White Cloud? I thought she perished in the fire. My brother and Swift Horse went looking for her . . ."

Alan gestured with his head toward the door.

"The horse is outside," he grumbled. "I brought your white mare home to you. Now I wish I'd kept it for myself. A man never has too many horses."

He glared first at Edward James and then at Marsha, then turned and stamped from the building.

Marsha felt a cold chill throughout her body. She hugged herself and visibly shivered as she looked slowly at Edward James, who was gazing lovingly down at her.

"He'll not bother you again," he said, gently drawing her into his embrace. Marsha clung to him, her eyes still on the closed door, and stiffened even more inside when she heard Alan Burton ride away in a hard gallop on his steed.

She seemed to have stirred up a hornet's nest. She deeply regretted having crossed paths with Alan Burton.

Had she remained at the trading post that day of the fires, and waited for a more opportune time to get someone to listen to her about Swift Horse's one-eyed friend, she wouldn't have put her brother in the position of having come face-to-face with a man he abhorred, nor would she have him to fear now.

As it was, she now had not only the one-eyed renegade to be afraid of, but also the cowkeeper.

She knew that she hadn't seen nor heard the last of this man. He seemed the determined sort, and he had obviously singled her out to be the next woman in his life.

She truly feared their next confrontation.

Chapter 13

Best and brightest, come away—
Fairer far than this fair day,
Which, like thee, to those in sorrow
Comes to bid a sweet good-morrow.
        —Percy Bysshe Shelley

Marsha worked quickly with her chores, glad that she had her strength back after her horrible ordeal. Her throat and lungs still ached, but not unbearably. Her parents had always said that she was the strongest girl they had ever known, despite her tiny frame.

Even when she had had bad colds that would incapacitate most people, she had been able to bounce back as good as new after only one day of having been made to stay in bed.

Today was a special day at the Creek village, and she was glad to feel well enough to join them in the council house.

Although her brother would be working at the trading post, he had told her that he thought it

would be all right if she joined the Wind Clan of
Creek on their special day, when they celebrated
the first buck killed this hunting season, although there were some things about it that
might cause her stomach to feel weak.

This special buck had been kept aside and
unskinned, for the special ceremony. Marsha
looked forward to this ceremony at the huge
council house, because she knew that she would
be able to see Swift Horse again, and this time in
his full capacity as chief. He would be presiding
over the ceremony.

The ceremony was to be held at midmorning,
which was quickly approaching. She had seen
several Creek people walking toward the council
house already. She had decided to wait until only
moments before the ceremony to go herself, for
she would be going there alone and would want
to stay far at the back so that no one would notice her.

Truth be told, all that she truly wanted from
this day was to be able to see Swift Horse again,
and see him presiding over the ceremony as
chief. Since he had brought her home after he
had taken her from Alan Burton, she had not
been able to get him off her mind.

She was smitten, and she had to rationalize
why.

Was it because he was so breathtakingly handsome? Or was it because he was a great chief—a leader? Or did she truly have feelings that went deeper than that?

After today, she hoped to have the answers she so badly needed, for she was in this village to stay, and she needed to get her head on straight about how she should feel about these people's chief.

Her heart seemed to miss several beats when she heard the voice of the man she had just been thinking about out in the store. He was asking Edward James about her! He wanted to know how she was, before he went on to the council house for the special ceremony.

She could hardly believe that he cared this much for her and her welfare, that he would inquire about her before he presided over an important ceremony; yet had it not been in his eyes every time he had looked at her that he cared?

Had it not been in his voice? Hadn't it been in the way he had held her so endearingly close when he had carried her on his lap away from the fire? And now, to have actually taken the time before the special ceremony to ask about her?

It made her insides melt with wonder all over

again about him, but this time, she knew why
she felt this way. She knew at this very moment
that she was not merely infatuated with this
man, nor simply grateful for what he had done
for her.

Her feelings centered around her heart, in that
she had fallen in love with this Creek chief, perhaps the very first time she had seen him.

She so badly wanted to go out into the store
and show him that she was all right—except for
the scar on her face, where she had been slightly
burned—but she was afraid that might be a bit
too forward. She would stay put and hope that
later on today she might be able to speak with
him—hopefully, alone.

A knock on the back door of the living quarters drew Marsha quickly around. She forked her
eyebrows when someone knocked again.

Wondering who it might be, she lifted the hem
of her skirt and started toward the door, then
stopped and thought of Alan Burton and how he
had shown such an interest in her.

If it was he, and he had come for his "reward"
for having saved her from the fire, she would not
know what to say to him.

She could never forget the look in his eyes
when he had talked about her and implied that

he wanted to court her since he no longer had a wife.

She started to back away from the door, her heart thudding inside her chest at the thought of it being the cowkeeper come to call, when a voice on the other side of the closed door proved her wrong.

It wasn't the cowkeeper after all. It was Abraham.

Sighing with relief, Marsha hurried to the door and opened it. She heaved a heavy sigh when she saw what Abraham had in his arms: It was the fawn that she had tried to rescue.

"Ma'am, I thought you might want to see the fawn this mornin' and see that it is farin' well," Abraham said, lovingly stroking the tiny animal's back as the fawn stared at Marsha with its wide, dark eyes. "And do you see? I have its leg in a splint and bandaged. It can get around all right now."

"Oh, Abraham, thank you so much for helping the sweet animal," Marsha said, glad when he held it out for her to take.

She held her arms out as he eased the fawn into them. She held it close and smiled down into its still-watchful eyes. "You dear," she murmured. "Had I not seen you . . ."

"Hush with talk such as that," Abraham softly

encouraged. "The fawn was saved and will soon be as fit as a fiddle. Its leg will heal good enough. One day it'll be among its own again."

"But not too soon, I hope," Marsha said, stroking the animal's back. "It wouldn't have a chance out there in the wild without its mother."

Abraham stood there silent for a while, then looked over his shoulder when he saw more people walking toward the huge council house, then gazed into Marsha's eyes. "Would it be too bold of me to ask if you're going to the ceremony?" he asked in a tone that was cautious.

"Yes, I plan to go," Marsha said, seeing how his eyes momentarily humbly lowered, then looked up at her again.

"Might I goes with you, ma'am?" Abraham asked, then visibly tightened. "Or am I bein' too bold to asks you, a white woman, such a question as that?"

"No, you aren't being too bold at all, and I'm glad you asked," Marsha hurried out. "I was dreading going by myself since my brother can't go." She smiled up at him. "Abraham, I would be delighted to have you as my escort," she murmured.

She hated the ignorance of many white people, how they could put themselves above anyone else, when everyone should be working together in this world to make it a better, equal place for all.

Marsha's thoughts were interrupted when she saw Soft Wind walking toward her, smiling from ear to ear. Abraham stepped aside as Soft Wind came up beside him, smiling a good morning to him and then at Marsha.

"Marsha, Edward James told me that you wanted to attend the ceremony this morning and were planning to go alone," Soft Wind murmured. "Would you like to attend with me? We could sit together."

Marsha looked quickly over at Abraham, whose eyes were humbly lowered, as though she could read his mind—that he thought she would rather go with Soft Wind than with him. She looked quickly at Soft Wind. "I would love to, but I have already promised Abraham I would go with him," she murmured, hearing a soft gasp coming from Abraham, and knowing why.

He was stunned that Marsha would choose him over Soft Wind! She quickly explained. "We could all go together," she hurried out, having accepted the fact now that her brother would be marrying this pretty maiden. "Would that be all right, Soft Wind?" She turned to Abraham. "Would that be all right, Abraham?"

His broad smile and dancing eyes were

enough response without his even saying anything, but then he hurried out, "Yes'm. I would
like that."

Soft Wind smiled. "I would like that, too," she
murmured. She turned to Abraham just as Marsha handed him the fawn. "The animal is sweet."
Then her smile waned. "But I do not think you
should take the fawn to the ceremony. When you
are there, you will see why I suggest this to you."

Marsha wondered what there could be about
the ceremony that would discourage having the
fawn there, and then she remembered: The first
buck kill was to be celebrated!

The animal that had been killed was going to
be there. It would not seem right to celebrate the
killing of one deer, while one that would one day
be as big, and surely then hunted, was there.

"I, too, advise you to take the fawn to your
home and leave it there," Marsha quickly said.
"Soft Wind and I will wait for you here, and then
we can go together to the council house."

"Yes'm," Abraham said, quickly nodding. He
turned and walked quickly away, the fawn held
lovingly in his arms.

Then Marsha stepped aside. "Come on inside,
Soft Wind, until Abraham returns," she murmured.

Soft Wind smiled and walked past Marsha,

then stopped and turned to her and smiled again. "Marsha, did Edward James tell you that we have decided to have the wedding ceremony in two sunrises?" she asked softly.

"Two . . . days . . . ?" Marsha said, her voice drawn, finding it hard to believe that her brother was marrying so soon.

"I'm happy for you," she murmured. "I know how happy you are making my brother."

She started to say something else even more positive—which she felt she owed Soft Wind because of how she had behaved earlier upon hearing the news—but stopped when several young braves ran past and into the forest, seemingly excited about something.

She quickly noticed that they were carrying bows, with quivers of arrows on their backs, all of which were smaller than those carried by grown adults.

"Where are they going?" she asked as she stepped outside again, watching. "Why are they so excited? Is it because of the council?"

"No, it has nothing to do with the council, for the young braves will not be there," Soft Wind said. "It is for adults only."

"Then where are they going armed?" Marsha asked, still watching as more of the young braves ran after those she had already seen.

"There is a target practice range not that far from our village where the youngsters practice shooting arrows from their bows," Soft Wind said matter-of-factly as she came outside and stood with Marsha. "It is good for them to shoot at targets other than living creatures until their skills at hunting are more honed."

Abraham stepped up to them. He was smiling broadly.

"We must go now," Soft Wind said, watching Marsha remove her apron and hang it from a peg on the wall, then close the door behind her.

"Will you explain the ceremony to me as it happens?" Marsha asked as they walked toward the huge council house, where people were filing in, one by one. She glanced over at Abraham. "It would be good for Abraham to know, too, since he plans to join the hunt one day."

"I will be glad to tell you both," Soft Wind said, smiling at Marsha and then past her at Abraham.

They went on into the council house. Marsha grabbed Soft Wind by an arm when Soft Wind started to go down to sit at the front of the people. "Please let's just sit here at the back," Marsha murmured. "I always feel that my presence disturbs some of your people."

"In time they will all accept you," Soft Wind said, then smiled knowingly at Marsha. "As my chieftain brother has accepted you."

Marsha hated it when she felt the heat of a blush rush to her cheeks!

Would he be able to read her feelings? Her mother had always told her that she wore her feelings on her face.

If she did so today, Swift Horse would know that she had fallen in love with him!

Chapter 14

Virtue, how frail it is!
Friendship, how rare!
—Percy Bysshe Shelley

Marsha was impressed by the huge council
house. It was made the same as the Creek people's homes, but much larger. Instead of wood
flooring, however, the floor was bare earth, and
in the center of the huge room a fire burned
within a circle of rocks, the smoke being drawn
through a hole in the roof that could be closed
during inclement weather.

All of the warriors who had been a part of the
hunt sat forward, facing the fire; the warriors
who had not participated this time and the
women and children sat behind them. Both
Chief Swift Horse and his shaman, Bright Moon,
sat on a platform facing everyone.

Marsha's pulse raced when she caught Swift
Horse glancing at her, holding his eyes on her

momentarily before looking away when a young brave brought a calumet pipe to him, and then another brave brought him fire for his pipe. Marsha was mesmerized at how the young brave placed the flames to the tobacco in the bowl of the pipe as Swift Horse sucked on the long stem, soon sending smoke upward.

After the two young braves were sitting again among the crowd, Swift Horse stood up and faced the east. "I blow my first puff of smoke to where the sun rises," he said, taking a drag from the pipe, blowing the smoke eastward. He repeated this process for the other cardinal points, then handed the pipe to Bright Moon, who also smoked from it, then handed the pipe to the warrior next to him, who passed the pipe on around the council house until all warriors had partaken of it.

When the pipe came back to Swift Horse where he again sat on the platform, he handed it to a young brave who came with a wooden case for it.

The pipe then taken away, Swift Horse rose again and faced everyone. "We are joined here today, as one heart and mind, to celebrate once again the first buck kill of the season, which will be sacrificed as our offering to the one above who allows this successful hunt," he said proudly. "This, too, is done as a thanksgiving for the recovery of health of those who among us are ill, and for our former success in hunting, so that the divine care and goodness may be still continued to our Wind Clan of Creek."

He motioned with a hand toward two warriors who had just come into the council house at the back carrying a large deer.

"Come forth," he said, motioning toward the warriors with his hands. "Pull the newly killed venison through the flames of the fire, both by the way of a sacrifice, and to consume the blood, life, or animal spirits of the beast."

Her eyes transfixed, Marsha watched as the deer that had been cleaned of the blood from the fresh kill was carried toward the huge fire, her thoughts returning momentarily to the small fawn that she had saved. She could not help but regret that one day it could be the first buck sacrifice. She tried not to think about that, for she knew the importance of these animals to the Creek.

Smoked meat was essential to Creek subsistence during the winter, and smoked and dried venison served as the main source of animal protein in the Creek diet throughout the year.

Not only were deer used for food to sustain the Creek throughout the cold winter months, the animals were also important in other ways. The deerskins were used for leggings, moccasins, fringe, binding, women's garments, breechcloths, shot pouches, string for bows, and household articles such as bedding, which required a tremendous number of hides.

She knew now that on the hunters' return to the village, they were expected to distribute some of their meat to the elderly and to those who were unable to hunt for themselves, as well as to the able-bodied who had remained in the village to protect it from enemies, and the conjurer who provided the medicines that attracted the deer.

Marsha felt a bitter sort of regret, and even shame, when she thought of how comfortably most whites lived. They most certainly did not have to depend on animals such as this for their existence! Yet she saw this way of life, which was simple and even beautiful to her, something she hoped to be a part of now that she knew her true feelings for Swift Horse.

She would move quickly from her home to his if he asked this of her, for she fell more in love with him every time she saw him.

If her brother could marry an Indian maiden, so could she marry a handsome, wonderful chief! Her face grew hot with a blush when she realized where her thoughts had taken her.

Her musings were interrupted when she saw the two warriors pull the buck slowly back and forth through the smoke of the lodge fire and then the flames, and then place the animal on a platform covered with a huge piece of buckskin.

Swift Horse stepped down from his platform, drew his knife from its sheath, and stood over the buck. Marsha watched him cut into the animal and take a huge fat piece of the meat from it, which her brother had said was called the milt, and held it over the fire.

"Today I offer the choicest part of the animal to the fire!" Swift Horse said, releasing the meat from his hands, dropping it down into the flames. Soon the smell of roasted venison filled the lodge as it baked in the flames.

Swift Horse then motioned to two other warriors to come forth. "It is time to fully dress the animal and pass parts of it around to those warriors who joined the hunt," he said thickly. "The pelt goes to the man whose first arrow sank into the flesh of the buck."

He sat down while all of the animal pieces were been passed around to those who deserved it, then watched as the remains were wrapped up in the huge piece of skin and taken from the council house.

"This concludes this council," Swift Horse said as he rose and stepped from the platform. Bright Moon stepped down beside him, then walked away and left the council house. Everyone else then rose and quietly left the council.

Marsha stepped out into the sun and saw how quickly Soft Wind ran away from her to the trading post where Edward James had stayed. Abraham had left earlier.

"And what did you think of your first council?" The masculine, deep voice caused Marsha to turn with a start.

She blushed when she found Swift Horse standing there, smiling at her.

"It was interesting," she murmured. "I find everything about you and your people interesting. I am fascinated, in fact. Your lives are so different from what I have ever known."

"It is a simple life," Swift Horse said softly. "But not always easy." He motioned with a hand toward the creek that ran snakelike along the edge of their village. "Come and sit with me? These days of lovely flowers, leaves, and warm air will soon be gone."

"I would love to," Marsha said, touched that he would take this time with her, when she knew that he had much more on his mind. She knew that the hunting season had just begun and that he would surely be leaving soon himself to join the hunt.

She felt uneasy to think about him being gone from the village. It was because he was his people's leader and protector. And she now felt as though he was her protector, as well. Had he not come for her when he had seen her leave the village, knowing the dangers she could have been putting herself in? Had he not brought her home safely to her brother?

They walked alongside the creek for a while beneath the colorful leaves, and when they came to a more private place, they stopped.

"I saw Abraham with you at the council," Swift Horse said as he and Marsha sat on a thick bed of colorful leaves that had fallen from the trees. "It is good that he shows such an interest in all that my people do. When he gets his full strength back, he will enjoy everything we Creek warriors enjoy, including the hunt, for from now on, he is a part of us."

"You are so kind to have allowed him to stay and live among your people," Marsha said. She pulled the skirt around her legs as she drew her knees up before her. "He is a kind man, someone whose life before now has surely been miserable."

"No one should be held as a slave," Swift Horse said, sitting down beside her. "There are many people of my color who have been slaves, too, of whites. And as people of my color move into what is called reservation life, by that, too, they are enslaved, for they are no longer able to roam the land as they wish. They are allotted a space and should they go farther, they are punished—sometimes even killed as though they are no more than that buck that was sacrificed today."

"I am so sorry for the injustices done to people of your color," Marsha murmured. "And of all color. There are many black slaves in Georgia where I was born and raised. My family was not as affluent as many are in Georgia, so no slaves were used at my father's farm. My father planted and harvested his own crops. That is how we survived."

"I am sad about your parents," Swift Horse said, his voice drawn.

"And yours," Marsha said, recalling how his parents had died. "It seems their fate was the same as my parents'. All were killed by renegades."

She paused, then turned to him. "But I know

exactly who killed mine," she said tightly. "The one-eyed man I saw in my brother's store. I am confident that he is the same man, Swift Horse, that you say is your best friend." She swallowed hard. "How could you call such a man a best friend when he is guilty of so many crimes?" she blurted out.

"You are mistaken," Swift Horse said thickly. "But I understand how you can be. There is more than one man whose eye has been removed due to warring."

"Just how well do you know this . . . friend?" Marsha asked guardedly.

"We have been friends since we were young braves anxious to walk in the moccasins of warriors," Swift Horse said, smiling over at her. "We have been together much. Do you not see that I would know an evil side of this man were there one to know? He is good, Marsha. My friend would give his life for me. He almost did."

"I want so badly to believe what you believe," Marsha murmured. "But I just can't see it in the same way." She visibly shuddered. "I will never forget that one eye leering at me right after he killed my parents. He . . . he . . . would have killed me, too, had it not been for those soldiers who had survived the ambush. He knew that if he stayed any longer, he would also die. He rode away quickly and was soon lost to my sight, as well as the soldiers'."

"I will help you find the one-eyed man who did you wrong," Swift Horse said softly. "But I must see to my chiefly duties first. Winter with its cold winds and snows will soon be upon us. It is important to get the hunt behind us, and then the harvesting of our crops is next. Once these things are finished, then I will gather together many warriors and will go on a different hunt—a hunt for the man who wronged you."

"You would do this for me?" Marsha asked, her eyes wide as she gazed into his, then she sighed heavily and looked away from him, for she knew the real killer would be overlooked.

Seeing her look away, and hearing her sigh, Swift Horse placed a gentle hand beneath her chin and drew her eyes back around to gaze into his. "I promise you today that the man who took your parents from you will pay for his crime," he said thickly. "I will be the one to make him pay. But you must trust me."

His eyes searched hers, making her feel weak with passion, something she had never felt before for any man. She felt dizzied by it.

She collected herself and slowly nodded. "Yes, I do," she murmured. "I do trust you."

Suddenly he had his arms around her, and she

found herself, as though by magic, twining her arms around his neck.

Their lips came together in a sweet kiss of bliss that made Marsha forget all ugliness of the world. While she was in this man's arms, everything was wonderful—was safe!

Then he withdrew from her, yet he still had his hands on her cheeks as he smiled into her eyes. "I have not allowed myself to love before, because my duties as chief have been foremost on my mind since I took over those duties upon the death of my father," he said thickly. "But I cannot help but love you."

He gazed intensely into her eyes. "I can see it in your eyes that you love me, too," he said. "I felt it in your kiss. Tell me. Tell me you love me."

"I do," Marsha murmured, sighing. "Oh, but I do. I felt something the first time I saw you, yet . . ."

"Yet you were afraid to feel something for a man whose skin is not the same color as yours— a man who is an Indian," he said, his voice drawn.

"It was not so much that I was afraid because you are an Indian. It was just that I wasn't sure of my feelings. For, you see, I have never loved before," she murmured. "I didn't want the attraction to be only because you were a powerful chief, whom everyone admires and loves. I wanted to be sure it was true love, and not infatuation."

"And you are certain now?" he asked, placing his arms around her waist again, drawing her closer.

"Oh, so very," she said, her breath captured in another kiss as his lips came to hers. She felt as though she were floating above herself, she was so taken by the kiss and his embrace. She knew now that everything in her life had changed, for love had taken center stage!

At this moment in time, even the memory of her parents' death seemed to have faded to the farthest recesses of her mind.

"I love you," she murmured against his lips as he slowly brushed them against hers now, not so much in a kiss, but a caress.

"My heart no longer belongs solely to my people," he whispered back. "It is yours, too, forever and ever."

She looked into his eyes, stunned that this was truly happening!

Chapter 15

When to the sessions of sweet silent thought
I summon up remembrance of things past,
I sigh the lack of many a thing I sought.
                    —William Shakespeare

Marsha was just pulling an apple pie from her oven when she heard a scream that almost made her drop the pie pan. She quickly placed her pie on the windowsill to cool, then rushed to the door and opened it.

A part of her was afraid to go on outside, for it was a woman's scream that she had heard.

She yanked off her apron, tossed it over her shoulder, and then walked outside just in time to see Bright Moon rushing to Soft Wind's cabin.

"Soft Wind . . ." she gasped, her eyes widening when she now saw Swift Horse hurrying into the cabin that sat beside his own.

Marsha ran and joined the crowd that had gathered. She edged closer to another woman

that she had become acquainted with and who
was one of Soft Wind's best friends.

"What's wrong?" Marsha asked as she gazed
questioningly into Red Flower's dark eyes.
"What happened?"

"Some young braves did not go to where they
are supposed to go when they practice shooting
their arrows," Red Flower murmured. "Instead
they were in the forest just behind Soft Wind's
lodge. An arrow . . . it . . . came through one of
Soft Wind's open windows."

"You say an arrow came through a window?"
Marsha gasped. "Does that mean that . . . that . . .
Soft Wind was injured by that arrow?"

Red Flower's eyes lowered, then rose again,
tears streaming from them. "Yes, that is what I
found too hard to say," she said, her voice breaking.

"Lord, no," Marsha said, turning when she
heard footsteps coming up behind her in a hard
run.

When she saw that it was Edward James, she
reached a hand out for him, but he wasn't even
aware that she was there. His eyes were on Soft
Wind's open front door.

He rushed inside just as Bright Moon stepped
outside and faced everyone. What the shaman
held made gasps ripple through the crowd, for it

was two halves of an arrow, both dripping with blood.

Marsha felt instantly ill to her stomach at the sight, for she knew that he had taken that arrow from Soft Wind's body! Flashes of that day when her parents were murdered by deadly arrows came to Marsha, making her feel suddenly dizzy.

Red Flower saw Marsha weave back and forth, and grabbed for her, placing an arm around Marsha's waist as they listened to what the village shaman had to say.

"I know that you are eager to know Soft Wind's condition," he said to the people. "A young brave's arrow went astray, flew through Soft Wind's open window, and sank into her left shoulder. It is not a mortal wound, but one that will require much attention and time for healing. But she is going to be all right. The wound has been medicated. Now all she needs is rest."

He looked slowly around the crowd. "Return to your homes," he suggested. "Now that you know that all will be well with Soft Wind, you can go about your daily activities."

Marsha saw the shaman's brow furrow into an angry scowl as a young brave was ushered through the crowd and stopped before him.

"My son Four Leaves," Sharp Nose said, holding the young brave by an arm. "He has come to apologize for not having gone to the practice range where he should have been."

Bright Moon sighed heavily, and being a man of good nature and forgiveness, he placed a gentle hand on the young man's shoulder. "Young brave, you have something to say?" he asked blandly.

Four Leaves's eyes lifted and wavered as he looked into Bright Moon's. "I am sorry," he gulped out. "I did not follow my father's teachings. I am sorry that my arrow went astray and . . . and . . . harmed Soft Wind."

Bright Moon stepped aside and gestured toward the door. "I accept your apology, but someone else needs it, too. Soft Wind is waiting for you," he said thickly. "Apologize, then go to your home and say prayers that will bring comfort into your own heart."

The child nodded, then ran inside. Everyone waited for him to come out again, and when he did, he was smiling broadly. "She forgave me," he said, gazing up at Bright Moon. Four Leaves then looked slowly over at his father, who was still angry at his son for the wrong that he had done. "Father, she . . . forgave . . . me," he gulped out. "Bright Moon forgave me. Do . . . you . . . ?"

Sharp Nose scowled for a moment longer, then bent to his knees and grabbed Four Leaves into his arms. "Yes, I forgive you, but you must never disobey again," he said thickly.

"I never shall," Four Leaves sobbed. "I promise, *ahte*, father. I promise."

Sharp Nose lifted his son into his arms, and with his chin held proudly high, walked through the crowd toward his cabin. Then all attention turned to Swift Horse as he emerged from the cabin.

"My sister will be well soon," he reassured. "But her wedding has to be postponed due to her injury."

Gasps rippled through the crowd, for everyone knew of Soft Wind's upcoming nuptials and had approved of them, for all approved of Edward James being her husband.

Edward James stepped outside and came to Marsha, interrupting her thoughts. "Marsha, Soft Wind is asking for you," he said thickly. "She wants you to sit with her while I return to my work at the store and her brother goes into council with his warriors."

"Me?" Marsha asked, her eyes widening. "She . . . wants . . . me? She asked for me?"

"Yes, you," Edward James said, smiling. "Will you come? Will you sit with her?"

Marsha recalled the food she had left cooking on her stove, and the pie that she had left on the windowsill to cool, then smiled back at her brother. "Yes, I would love to," she murmured. "But, Edward James, will you take the food off the stove for me and the pie from the windowsill? Will you bring both here? We shall share our dinner with Soft Wind and Swift Horse. You know that I always make enough for an army."

Then she grew solemn. "But perhaps she is too ill to eat," she said, her voice breaking.

"She needs rest, but she also needs nourishment that will help her health improve, so no, she is not too ill to eat, and will even welcome it," Edward James said. He turned to Swift Horse. "I will bring food back for all of us."

Swift Horse nodded and smiled, then turned to Bright Moon. "Will you stay?" he asked softly.

"I have much to do, so, no, I had best not delay any longer," he said. He placed a hand on Swift Horse's shoulder. "Your sister is fortunate. The arrow could have inflicted a mortal wound."

"I know," Swift Horse said, nodding, not seeing how Marsha's color left her face at the news.

Bright Moon gave Swift Horse a quick embrace, then turned and walked away.

"It was that close?" Marsha asked, searching Swift Horse's eyes. "She could have died?"

"Yes, it was that close," Swift Horse said solemnly.

"I'm so sorry," Marsha murmured, then walked inside with Swift Horse.

She went to Soft Wind's bedroom, where a soft fire burned low on the grate of a stone fireplace. Seeing Soft Wind so pale and how the wound on her shoulder was covered with some sort of white, pasty medicine made Marsha's heart go out to her. She knelt down beside Soft Wind's thick pallet of furs and blankets and placed a soft hand on her brow.

"You will be all right," she reassured.

"My shaman reassured me of that," Soft Wind said softly.

"I'm sorry that you have to postpone the wedding," Marsha said, reaching a hand for one of Soft Wind's, and taking it. "Truly I am."

"I know," Soft Wind said, nodding. "It will not have to be too long a wait, but I would like for the wound to be healed before I spend the first night in my new husband's bed."

Marsha blushed at those words, knowing the meaning behind them, then turned her eyes quickly to the door when Edward James came into the room with a young brave. Edward James carried the pot of stew and the child carried the pie.

"I shall get the eating utensils," Swift Horse said, hurrying from the room.

Edward James sat the pot on the table and took the pie and placed it there, too, then thanked the young brave, who hurried from the cabin. He knelt on the other side of Soft Wind's bed. "Do you feel like eating?" he asked softly, gently stroking her brow with a hand.

"How can I not when it all smells so good?" Soft Wind said, giggling.

Soon they were all eating. Edward James fed Soft Wind, who was propped up onto soft wrappings of doeskin. She ate only a few bites, then closed her eyes. "Enough," she said, her voice failing. "Sleep. I . . . need . . . sleep."

Edward James looked quickly at Swift Horse.

"Bright Moon fed her an elixir that would make her sleep," he said. "We must leave her now."

"Edward James, I know that you have work to do, as do you, my brother," Soft Wind said as her eyes just barely opened. She looked from her brother to the man she loved. "Go. Marsha will sit with me as I sleep." She turned slow eyes to Marsha. "Will you sit with me?"

"Yes, for as long as you want me to," Marsha said, touched that the woman would ask this of her. She truly felt that she and Soft Wind were friends now. Perhaps they might even be best friends one day.

"We shall go then," Swift Horse said, rising.

Edward James bent low and brushed a soft kiss across Soft Wind's brow as Marsha stood and walked Swift Horse to the door in the living room.

"Again, I am so sorry about Soft Wind, that something like this happened," she murmured.

"It is because of the foolishness of a young brave who now knows the meaning of being careless," Swift Horse said.

He looked quickly over his shoulder and saw that Edward James was lingering a moment longer beside his sister's bed. He took that opportunity to sweep his arms around Marsha's waist and bring her up against him.

"My woman, thank you for caring," he said, gazing into her eyes.

"It is not hard to care for your sister or you," Marsha murmured.

Swift Horse glanced over his shoulder again, and seeing that Edward James was still lingering at Soft Wind's bedside, he gazed again into Marsha's violet eyes.

"Show me how much you care," he said huskily.

Almost dizzied by her feelings for this man,

she leaned up and twined her arms around his neck and pressed her lips against his. Soon they were kissing passionately, their bodies straining together, until they heard someone clearing his voice behind them.

Startled that her brother had caught her being this intimate with Swift Horse, Marsha blushed and stepped quickly away from the Creek chief.

"Perhaps your marriage should take the place of mine that has to be postponed," Edward James teased, his eyes dancing as he looked from his sister to Swift Horse.

"Perhaps . . ." Swift Horse said, bringing Marsha's eyes quickly to him.

For a moment there was a complete silence, then Edward James broke the spell as he stepped up past Swift Horse and Marsha. "I must get back to work," he said, smiling devilishly at them as he left the cabin.

Swift Horse again drew Marsha into his arms. "It is something to think about," he said thickly. "A marriage soon between us." Then he stepped away from her and left, leaving her absolutely stunned and in awe of what had just happened.

She touched her lips with her fingers where Swift Horse's lips had just been. "Did this truly happen?" she whispered, stepping quickly to the door to watch Swift Horse walk toward the huge council house where he was to meet with his warriors again in council.

She felt strangely weak in the knees and she could not get past the fact that he might truly be serious about marrying her.

"Can this truly happen?" she whispered.

Chapter 16

Come slowly, Eden!
Lips unused to thee,
Bashful, sip thy jasmines,
As the fainting bee.
—Emily Dickinson

The day was exceptionally warm for the month of October. The wind blew softly through the window beside the bed where Soft Wind lay in a soft, peaceful sleep.

"It is still Indian summer," Marsha whispered to herself as she rocked slowly in a chair beside Soft Wind's bed, crocheting. She paused with her work to gaze at Soft Wind. Marsha was taking turns with the other women of the village sitting with Soft Wind until she was able to leave her bed.

"Sleep sweetly," Marsha whispered, reaching over to smooth a fallen lock of Soft Wind's hair back from her eyes.

"She sleeps, I see." A voice now so familiar to Marsha spoke up behind her.

She turned and smiled at Swift Horse as he came into the bedroom in his fringed buckskins, his hair long and loose today, with its usual lone feather hanging from a coil of the hair.

"Yes, she is sleeping," Marsha said, laying her sewing on the bedside table.

She wasn't quite used to how her heart could change so rapidly from beating its normal rate inside her chest to something erratic and thumping, which always happened when she first saw Swift Horse again after not having seen him for several hours.

She smiled and rose from the chair as he came to stand over the bed beside her.

"My sister's wound will soon be well and she can resume her plans for marriage," he said, reaching down and placing his palm on Soft Wind's brow. "Good. She still has no fever. That means that her body is strong enough to fight back the heat that I felt around her wound last night."

"Yes, I, too, thought she might have an infection," Marsha murmured, standing so close to Swift Horse now, she felt as though her entire being was one huge throb, her excitement to be with him again was so intense.

"I have brought Pretty Doe to sit with my

sister so that you can leave," Swift Horse said, turning to Marsha.

She looked over her shoulder and saw the lovely maiden standing in the living room, waiting, a basket of beading materials in her right hand. Then she smiled up at Swift Horse. "Thank you," she murmured. "I guess I should go home to the chores that await me. I still haven't made the bread that I had planned to make two days ago."

"Can it wait one more day?" he asked, searching her eyes with his. "I have some spare time on my hands. I would like to spend that time with you."

"You . . . would . . . ?" Marsha asked, her eyes widening as she gazed more intensely into his.

"It is a good day for a ride," he said. "Can you spare the time to share a ride with me?"

"I would love to go with you," Marsha said, grabbing up her crochet work and placing it in her sewing basket. "It has been a while since I have gone riding for relaxation. Since my arrival here, I have had other things on my mind."

"I believe riding for pleasure will help lift some of that burden from your heart," Swift Horse said, leaving the bedroom with her. He turned to Pretty Doe. "When my sister awakens she will be ready to eat. You will find food warming on the stove in the kitchen."

Pretty Doe smiled and nodded, then went into Soft Wind's bedroom.

Marsha stepped outside into the warmth of the day with Swift Horse. "I shall be only a moment," she murmured as she walked with Swift Horse toward his cabin. "I will go and tell Edward James our plans, then I shall meet you here shortly on my horse."

White as the puffiest cloud one could see on a summer's day, White Cloud was grazing in Marsha's brother's corral to the right of where she had established a clothesline for use on wash day.

"Do you need help in saddling your steed?" Swift Horse asked, not certain just how much she knew about riding horses or preparing them for riding.

"I will do fine," she murmured, then smiling, walked away from him. She knew that he doubted she knew much about horses. She would be glad to prove how wrong he was.

And it was wonderfully exciting to even think about being on a horse again simply for enjoyment. When her parents had died, so much of her spirit had died with them, and she was glad to feel it reviving within her. It was very exciting

for her to think about being on White Cloud
again.

She hurried home, and after telling her
brother about her plans and seeing his approval
in his smiling eyes, she ran to the corral, saddled
White Cloud, and began her ride alongside Swift
Horse.

She laughed softly when some of the tangled
webs of autumn got caught in her hair as they
rode from the village.

"Sometimes, of late, it seems the world is one
huge cobweb," she said, gazing over at Swift
Horse just as he brushed some of those same
webs from his long, sleek black hair.

"It is one of the mysteries of life," he said,
smiling. His gaze lingered on her and how she
sat so straight in her saddle, her feet resting comfortably in the stirrups.

She held the reins masterfully and steadily,
and he saw how occasionally she would stroke
the horse's neck, as though it were a special
friend to her.

"Her name is White Cloud," Marsha said,
having caught him seeing her stroking her mare
so lovingly. "She has been my horse since she
came into the world. I am so glad to have been
able to bring her to Kentucky with me after we

had to sell off so many other horses before set-ting out on our journey."

"Yes, I *can* see how familiar you are with the horse, and how much you care for it," Swift Horse said, pleased to learn something else about her.

"Back in Georgia, my family had so many horses, sometimes I would lose count," Marsha said, lost in thought. "Many of my friends raced horses. I didn't choose to. I thought it cruel, how they pushed the horses beyond their limit in an effort to win this race or that."

"Your love for the horse is very evident," Swift Horse said, nodding. "And I feel your sense of pride in how you talk of it. I admire you for not having gone the route of the others, for I, too, do not push any horse too hard unless forced to."

"White Cloud needs this outing today as much as I do," Marsha said. "The last time I rode her was a day I'd rather not remember."

"You are having trouble getting that day from your mind," Swift Horse said, gazing over at the faint scar on her cheek where the fire had burned her, so glad that it *was* all but gone.

"Yes, but I will get past it," Marsha said, her voice breaking. She smiled softly over at him. "I am doing much better now."

"I can see in your eyes and your smile that you are," Swift Horse said. "Come. I will show you a place that will help lift more of the burden from your heart. When you are there, all bad is erased, and only good is left to marvel at."

"What I have seen of your land so far is beautiful," Marsha said, making a sharp turn left, following Swift Horse's lead.

"Our Creek country is noble and fruitful," Swift Horse said, looking straight ahead as they rode slowly and carefully through the forest, weaving around this tree and that.

"All Creek belong to a totemic clan. My own people's clan is the Wind, so named because a great fog had once shrouded this area and my ancestors were the first to emerge into the clear wind. Ours is one of the most powerful clans associated with a natural phenomenon—which is the wind. A clan is the cornerstone of Creek justice."

"Your sister's name has a part of your clan's name in it," Marsha said, drawing his eyes momentarily to hers once again.

"It was because she was born into a powerful family of chiefs," Swift Horse said, smiling proudly at Marsha. "She, in truth, is a Creek princess, but because she does not wish to appear to any of our people as more special than they, she does not allow me or anyone to refer to her as princess."

"I am discovering more and more just how special she is," Marsha murmured. "Does my brother know her status as princess?"

"I told him, but I also told him never to call her that, for she would be disappointed in me for having told your brother," Swift Horse said. "But since he is going to be her husband, I feel he should know everything about her. It is best never to have secrets when one becomes husband and wife."

"Then will she finally tell him herself?" Marsha asked, her eyes questioning him.

"In her own time, yes, she will tell him," Swift Horse said, nodding.

Suddenly Marsha was aware of a rushing sound that was unfamiliar to her. She gave Swift Horse a questioning look, which he understood.

"We are almost there," he said, smiling.

"We are almost where?" she asked, even more aware of the rushing sound, which now sounded like splashing water to her, yet much more deafening than any she had ever heard before.

They rode free of the forest and Marsha saw a place that she would describe as nothing less than a paradise. It was a waterfall, with lovely flowers growing on each side, and a rainbow amidst the splash of the water.

"Come and let us sit and talk," Swift Horse said, taking her reins. He swung himself from his horse and helped Marsha from her saddle. He tied the reins together on a low tree limb, and they both sat down on a boulder and watched the waterfall rushing downward to where it finally splashed into the river far below.

"I find the falls to be medicinal, sacred waters," Swift Horse said, his eyes watching the rush of the water downward. "When I am here I feel my own spirit strengthened and I also feel the spirits of my ancestors who have come here before me, to meditate and pray."

He gazed over at her and took one of her hands in his. "I wanted to share this special place with you," he said. "Although the wound on your face caused by the fire is all but healed, it is your soul that I feel needs to be comforted. I want to help erase that terrible day from inside your heart and mind, as best it can be erased. I know that your parents' death will always haunt you. I would like you to find acceptance and peace."

"I feel so many things while I am sitting here with you," Marsha murmured. "I do feel peace inside my heart, and I feel as though I might be able to finally accept my parents' deaths. Yet there is something inside me that will never go away until ... that ... man ... ."

He purposely interrupted her, in order to cut short her thoughts on the evil man while they were there together in such a special place. "He, too, will one day be only a bad memory," he reassured. "It will fade until you will no longer be burdened with the memory of what he did."

"I shall never forget his face," Marsha said, visibly shuddering.

"That, too, will fade," Swift Horse reassured. "And when he is captured and made to pay for the crime, your heart will no longer ache for vengeance. It will finally be achieved."

She so badly wanted to tell him that until she convinced everyone that the killer was the man whom Swift Horse called his best friend, she would never be able to rest.

"Please tell me more about your people," she pleaded because she did not want to think of the one-eyed man any more today. This was a special, private time with Swift Horse, the man she now knew that she would adore and love forever.

"Sitting here, where I feel spirits all around us,

it will be my pleasure to teach you about my people," Swift Horse said, slowly looking around him at the autumn leaves, at the flowers, and at the filmy foam of water as it cascaded down from above, to the river below.

"*Esaugeta Emissee,* the master of breath, is a kind spirit who watches over my Creek people," Swift Horse explained, gazing over at Marsha and seeing her interest by how she leaned forward, listening. "He is surrounded by a few lesser spirits. Some animals such as the wolf and rattlesnake occupy positions of deference and honor in my people's culture. Magic permeates much of our culture."

"Magic?" Marsha said, her eyes widening. "What kind of magic?"

As they sat there so attentive to each other, they were unaware of another presence. One Eye lurked close by behind bushes, watching and plotting. He had to stop this thing between Swift Horse and the white woman soon. He had a plan, but he had to make certain that Swift Horse could never discover that it was his best friend who had killed the woman. One Eye treasured the friendship and loyalty between him and Swift Horse too much to chance losing it.

He crawled away from his hiding place and then ran stealthily beneath the trees until he reached where he had left his steed. He led his horse away on foot, making certain it walked on a thick cushion of leaves so that his presence would not be detected.

Chapter 17

Nymph of the downward smile, and sidelong glance,
In what diviner moments of the day
Art thou most lovely?

—John Keats

Swift Horse continued to teach Marsha about his people, encouraged by her occasional soft gasps of wonder.

"Charms, bad-luck omens, and mythical creatures such as the great horned snakes and tie snakes occupy niches in the thinking of all Creeks," he said, wincing when he thought that he had heard a movement behind him, then relaxing again. "Tie snakes are friendly creatures who have towns under the waters of creeks and swamps, and who occasionally capture a Creek for the purpose of showing him hospitality."

"They actually capture . . ." Marsha gasped, her color paling.

Swift Horse placed a comforting arm around her waist and drew her close to him. "Do not fret over such things," he reassured. "Although it is said these things are true, in most of my people's minds and hearts they know that the tales are mythical."

"Then I don't have to worry about tie snakes?" Marsha asked, swallowing hard.

"I was wrong to tell you such things," he said, seeing that he had truly put fear into her heart when what he wanted was to make her forget the other things that were ugly. In a way, it did seem that he had succeeded, at least for the moment.

"Even with fear in your eyes you are beautiful," he said, his voice drawn. "But you are more beautiful when it is not there." He bent low and softly kissed her lips. "Let me kiss the fear away."

Marsha found it hard to concentrate at all, as he swept her closer to him and kissed her with more intensity, the passion strong between them. Then, breathless from these new feelings that were overwhelming her, Marsha moved her lips from his.

"I feel so many things," she murmured, gazing into his eyes. "But nothing akin to fear." She searched his eyes and placed a gentle hand on his cheek. "Swift Horse, how can someone love as quickly as I have fallen in love with you?"

"How can I answer that when I feel the same for you and as quickly?" he said huskily.

"But you are a powerful, noble, and knowledgeable man," Marsha said softly. "I see you as a man who knows everything."

"This thing called love is new to me, for as I have told you, I have never loved a woman before," Swift Horse said, framing her face between his hands and bringing her lips ever so close, yet not close enough to kiss. "But soon I will know everything there is to know about this thing called love, for each moment that I am with you, you teach me more about it."

"As you are teaching me," Marsha said, the breath catching in her throat when he brought his lips down onto hers again, then moved them as quickly away.

He could hardly control his heartbeats, nor his passion, and knew that it was time to return her home, or they might be drawn far past just kisses, and he respected her too much to go that way, just yet.

"Your brother will be concerned if we remain gone for much longer," he said thickly. "I will return you home now. He can see that I am an honorable man in doing so."

"You are honorable in all that you do, but yes, I believe we should leave, too, for my heart is pounding so hard, if it gets much harder, I will not be able to think, much less ride White Cloud," Marsha said, seeing the danger in their staying alone like this for much longer. She had strange new feelings within her, chief among them a hunger she had never known before.

"I will take you home to your bread-making," Swift Horse said, chuckling as he helped her up from the rock.

He could not help himself, though. He needed her in his arms at least one more moment, to sustain him until they were together again.

But this time he did not kiss her. He just gazed adoringly onto her face and into her eyes, which were the color of wild violets in the spring.

"You are more beautiful than any flower, butterfly, or sunset that I have ever known before in my life," he said huskily. "I shall always love you. Always."

"As I shall you," she murmured, then walked hand-in-hand with him to their horses.

When they were riding toward home, there was more peace within Marsha than she had felt since before leaving Kentucky. This man did have a way of righting wrongs within her heart. She knew that she had found the man she was destined to meet and marry.

Marsha caught him watching her as she glanced over at him.

"I do love you," Swift Horse said.

"I have surely loved you forever, even before I knew you," Marsha said softly. "I do love you, Swift Horse."

"The day your parents chose to move to my land, surely I knew it already inside my heart that we would meet and fall in love," Swift Horse said. "I do remember not so long ago, when the sun was still high and hot during the summer months, and a vision came to me. In it were eyes such as yours, and a smile. That vision was you, my woman. You."

She was stunned that he had seen this in a vision, long before they knew each other existed. That was proof that it was meant to be—that fate had drawn them together!

Chapter 18

Shadow of annoyance
Never came near thee:
Thou lovest, but ne'er knew love's sad satiety.
—Percy Bysshe Shelley

"Are you all right?" Edward James asked as he slipped a fringed buckskin jacket on. "Sis, you've seemed flushed since your ride with Swift Horse. Do you have a fever?"

Marsha placed the last of the dishes in the cupboard, untied her apron and hung it on a peg on the wall, then gave her brother a big, warm hug.

"I'm fine," she murmured. "It was just the sun. And you know how warm the weather can get during the days of Indian summer. That's all, big brother. I just got a bit too much sun."

She pressed her cheek against his chest, but her mind was on another man who had embraced her today—who had kissed her and declared such love for her.

She smiled a secret smile—for, in truth, it was not the sun or the warmth of the day at all that had brought such color to her cheeks.

It was Swift Horse.

For the first time since that terrible day of the ambush she was excited about something and had a renewel of hope that her life could be good and happy again.

"But you enjoyed the outing, didn't you?" Edward James asked, gently taking her by the shoulders and easing her away from him so that they could look into each other's eyes—his blue, hers violet, one color for each of their parents.

"You know that I did," Marsha said, laughing softly when she saw her brother's expression change from questioning to knowing. She eased from his arms and went to stand before a mirror that was on the wall above the washbasin.

"I had hoped for this day," Edward James said, reaching and running a hand lovingly through her thick golden tresses. "When I would see that laughter in your eyes again. Tonight I see even more than that. You are in love. The same as I, your heart has been stolen by an Indian."

She lifted the hem of her skirt with her hands and spun around, giggling.

"My Lord, big brother, I *am* in love," she said, now stopping and smiling into his eyes. "I had begun to wonder if I was going to be a spinster, for until now I have never felt anything akin to love for any man. Isn't it a wonderful feeling, Edward James, to truly be in love?"

Edward James threw his head back in a fit of laughter, for it *was* good to see his sister this happy, whereas even only a few days ago, he had never thought he would experience seeing her this way again. When she was happy, he was— twofold!

"Yes, it's a wonderful feeling," Edward James said, reaching for her hands and taking them in his. "I'm so happy for you."

"As I am for you," Marsha murmured. She lowered her eyes for a moment, then looked up at him again. "I'm going to marry Swift Horse, Edward James. He . . . he . . . asked me today."

Edward James's eyes widened. "Actually?" he asked.

"Yes, actually," Marsha said, then led him from the kitchen to the living room. "You'd best grab up those flowers, big brother," Marsha said, indicating the bouquet on the table. "You have a lovely maiden anxiously awaiting your arrival."

"Will you be seeing Swift Horse tonight?" Edward James asked, stepping away from her and grabbing the flowers.

"No," she murmured. "He spent the full day

with me, so tonight he plans to meet with some of his warriors in council."

"Do you know the reason for this council?" Edward James asked, forking an eyebrow. "He never mentioned anything about it to me."

"It might have to do with our most ardent enemy," Marsha said, this time somewhat solemnly.

"Who is . . . ?" Edward James said, searching her eyes.

"You know without me having to say it," Marsha said tightly. "Lord, Edward James. Who *is* our enemy? The man with the one eye who is none other than One Eye, Swift Horse's best friend."

Edward James sighed heavily. "Please forget that notion, sis," he said tightly. "One Eye is not the man who did that terrible deed to our parents. It is another man with one eye. Please believe this. I know One Eye well. He is a gentle, caring man who lives for peace, not for murdering innocent people."

"How can I get anyone to believe me?" Marsha suddenly cried, throwing her hands in the air with frustration. She turned to Edward James. "One day you will all see how right I am," she murmured as she stepped up to him. "If I have to go and find him myself, I shall."

Edward James gave her a woebegone look, sighed, then gazed at the door that led out to the back of the cabin, which was not that far from the dark forest.

He turned and gave Marsha a wavering look. "Sis, double lock that door while I'm gone," he said. "I'm going out the front way, through the store."

"And so even *you* are worried about One Eye, and won't admit it," Marsha said, walking him to the door that led into the store. "Or else why are you concerned about locks on the door?"

"There are more evil men out there besides the man with the one eye," Edward James said glumly. "There is Cowkeeper, or do you forget his interest in you? I imagine he has had a hard time getting you off his mind, and he just might think he does own you and will come for you."

He gazed at the door, and then Marsha. "Just be sure not to let anyone in unless they identify themselves as someone you know," he said, opening the door to the store. "I shan't be long, sis. I don't want to tire Soft Wind too much. I'm anxious for her to get her strength back so that we can exchange our vows."

"Me too," Marsha said, going to him and giving him a soft kiss on the cheek. "Tell Soft Wind that I'm thinking about her. I plan to take my crochet work tomorrow and show her how the stitches are done."

"That's good, sis," Edward James said, smiling broadly. He went into the store as Marsha closed the door behind him.

She gazed at the lock on that door, then shrugged and left it undone, for she knew that no one ever entered the store without her brother being there. Sighing, Marsha went and sat down in a rocking chair before a softly burning fire in the fireplace. She lifted the crochet thread and placed it on her lap, then plucked the hook up and began crocheting, which she planned to do until she went to bed.

Her thoughts turned to Swift Horse and just what he might be planning in council. Hopefully it did all have to do with the one-eyed man. She expected him and his warriors to go on a search party for him, and when they discovered that there was only one evil one-eyed man in the area, they would give in and know that it was Swift Horse's pretend friend, One Eye.

Alan Burton shifted nervously in his saddle, then grinned when he saw Edward James hurry from the front door of the trading post and head in the direction of Soft Wind's cabin. Alan had heard about her mishap, and smiled at his own good fortune. He could count on Edward James leaving his house every evening to be with Soft Wind as she recuperated, which left Marsha alone and unprotected.

He edged his horse closer to the clearing and watched Edward James until he went into Soft Wind's cabin, then he rode out into the open, took his horse to the darkest side of the trading post, and dismounted. He secured the reins on a hitching rail, then after stopping long enough to look over his shoulder, he hurried into the store.

He smiled wickedly to himself at the foolishness of Edward James's truly believing everyone was too afraid to cross the threshold of his store because it was said that if they were found there, their life wouldn't be worth spit. Edward James would either shoot them on the spot, or capture them and take them to Fort Hill to hang.

Knowing that Edward James would be occupied for a good amount of time, Alan knew that he had the time to do as he wished tonight, and that was to take the lovely woman away and back to his home.

Edward James and Swift Horse might see him as the prime suspect for such an act since he had made such an issue over having saved her life, so he knew that his home would be the first place they would search when they discovered she was gone.

He had that problem solved. He had a room at his house that no one knew about, where he kept his money and valuable pelts. The room had no windows, and the only way into the room was a door that he had cleverly hidden behind a chifforobe that he kept wedged up against it.

"Yep, she'll be mine," he whispered to himself. He hoped by the time they gave up on finding her, he'd be long gone, for he had made an important decision the very night he had saved the beautiful woman.

He was going to leave these parts.

He was sorely tired of fighting with the Creek for land that he needed for his cows. He would go elsewhere. He would make a new beginning and he would have the most beautiful woman in the world finally accepting her fate enough to marry him. She would have no idea where he had taken her, so she would have no idea how to escape.

Marsha had just sat back down to resume her crocheting after having stopped to prepare herself a cup of hot tea. While waiting for it to cool, she rocked slowly back and forth, her crochet work on her lap, her eyes on the softly burning fire. She smiled as she thought of the wonders of the day.

"Swift Horse . . ." she whispered, even loving just the sound of his name as it came across her lips, lips that he had claimed today more than once in wondrous kisses.

A noise in the store caused Marsha to stop rocking and her hands to go to the arms of the chair. She started to get up to investigate, but smiled to herself when she heard nothing else.

Humming a soft song now, she resumed rocking, and felt a contentment she had not known for so long as she lifted her crochet work.

When she heard footsteps and then the door opening, Marsha smiled and didn't look up. "Big brother, did you forget something?" she asked softly.

"I'm not your big brother, but, yeah, I forgot something, all right," said a voice that was *not* Edward James's. "I forgot *you*."

Marsha dropped her work on the floor, everything scattering at her feet, and before she could scream, Alan had placed a gag in her mouth, then tied her wrists together.

"Come with Daddy," he said, laughing throatily. "We've some unfinished business, don't you know? You owe me, pretty lady. And I'm here to see that you give me everything that I ask of you."

Frightened terribly, Marsha could only see through a blur of tears as Alan Burton half dragged her toward the back door.

He held her tightly around her waist as he unlocked both locks, laughing at how she tried to kick and fight her way loose, then took her outside, where for a moment the moon fell down upon her and illuminated the fear in her eyes.

One Eye was on his horse in the dark shadows of the forest. He was watching all of this go down, then laughed to himself. Alan Burton had just done the tricky job of abducting Marsha Eveland for him. All blame would be cast on the cowkeeper, for One Eye knew that Swift Horse was the cleverest tracker of all Creek clans and he would trace his way up to the cowkeeper's ranch.

Of course, One Eye was a clever tracker, as well, and knew just how to hide the tracks he had made while watching the abduction taking place, and also those that he would make while going to the cowkeeper's ranch.

No one would ever suspect One Eye, and finally he would be rid of two nuisances in one night—the cowkeeper and the woman—and all evidence would point to it having been the cowkeeper who killed the lady, and the lady who killed the cowkeeper while trying to defend herself.

He laughed to himself as he started following Alan Burton and Marsha.

Chapter 19

Another time mine eye is my heart's guest,
And in his thoughts of love doth share a part.
—William Shakespeare

Swift Horse left Edward James sitting with his sister to go and talk with Marsha. But first he decided to drop in on Abraham, to make sure that his new friend wasn't left out of things. Swift Horse wanted him to feel like he was home—truly home.

He drew people to him, because he was such a likable man. It was hard for Swift Horse to envision this proud black man as a slave, being treated so poorly by his "owner," who had beaten Abraham almost to death with the nasty, deadly whip.

Swift Horse saw the lamplight in Abraham's cabin and knew that he was still awake. More than likely Abraham was sitting beside the fire with the fawn on his lap, as he did most evenings.

Swift Horse stepped up to the door and knocked, and Abraham's booming voice told him to come in.

Swift Horse went inside and found Abraham bent over a book, with a kerosene lamp on a table drawn close enough for him to read by. It was obvious that before Swift Horse entered, the man had been absorbed in the "talking leaves," which was what one of the Creek children had nicknamed books.

"Comes on in," Abraham said, placing a ribbon in the book to mark the last page that he had been reading. He set the book on the table and rose to greet Swift Horse, giving him a big hug.

"I'se got coffee brewin' over the fire," Abraham said, stepping away from Swift Horse. "Do you have time to sit and share coffee with me?"

"I always have time for you," Swift Horse said.

Abraham poured coffee into two tin cups and handed one to Swift Horse, then sat in a chair opposite him, a steaming cup of coffee in his hand.

"Do you see this book?" Abraham said, setting his cup aside and lifting the book from the table. The book seemed dwarfed in his massive hand as he held it out for Swift Horse to see.

"Yes, and are you enjoying it?" Swift Horse

asked as Abraham opened the book, pride shining in his eyes.

"Very much," Abraham said, nodding. "Marsha brought it to me when she found out that I could read. My mama sneaked books into our cabin at night when I was a child. She had been taught by a white friend who sneaked books to my mama and read to her by candlelight into the wee hours of the night. My mama taught me and I taught my own chillen from the very same book my mama taught me from."

Tears came to Abraham's dark eyes. "One evenin', as I was teachin' my chillen from that book," he said, his voice breaking, "my mastah caught me." He took the book and tore pages from it one at a time as he laughed at my despair. Then he held a candle to each page and let the flaming pages fall to the floor of my cabin. I had to stamp out that fire with my bare feet. I hated that man that night more than I can tells you."

He clutched the book to his heart and lowered his eyes. "It was a short while later that he killed my family and spared my life because I was such a big, healthy man, who could do the work of three men at his plantation."

"I am so sorry for all that you have had to endure," Swift Horse said, setting down his empty coffee cup.

"Your people have endured much, too," Abraham said, laying the book aside and gazing over at Swift Horse. "I heard tales of it when I lived in Florida land. The Seminole did not get treated as bad as I heard tell Indians up north and out west were being treated. 'Genocide' I believe is the word I heard used as a description of how it was when so many people of your skin color was killed."

"Yes, it is not always a kind world," Swift Horse said, although he did remember that not all white men took pleasure in mistreating the black community or those with red skin. He could not have a closer friend than Edward James.

Edward James was a better friend to Swift Horse now than even One Eye, who sometimes *did* seem to have changed from that young brave Swift Horse had known as a child.

Whenever Swift Horse thought about that change, Marsha's accusations against One Eye always came to mind.

Swift Horse wanted to believe in One Eye and not think that he could be anything akin to the renegade who killed Marsha's parents, but lately something about One Eye did make Swift Horse begin to wonder. Certainly Swift Horse was pay-ing more heed now to what One Eye said and did.

"I have received much pleasure in knowin' Edward James and Marsha, and their skin is white," Abraham said, seeming to have read Swift Horse's mind. "And I knew some kind whites back in Florida land, too. My mastah's wife had the same sweet sort of smile and voice that I have found in Marsha."

Abraham suddenly smiled. "She sneaked freshly baked cookies to my chillen time and time again," he said, lost for a moment in sweet memories."I misses her as I am sure she misses and worries 'bout me. After her husband killed my family, she sneaked out to my cabin and embraced me and told me she was so sorry."

They were interrupted when the fawn limped in from a back room, went to Abraham, and gazed up at him. "You want me to hold and rock you, don'tcha?" Abraham said, lifting the tiny thing into his arms. He smiled over at Swift Horse. "He thinks he's a real person. He likes being rocked." He laughed softly. "I even sing to him sometimes like I sang to my chillen when I rocked them to sleep at night."

"And so the fawn's leg is better, I see," Swift Horse said as he leaned over and stroked the animal's sleek fur. "He limps, but at least now he can get around on his own."

"I took many an injured animal into my cabin at night when the mastah couldn't see. I did what I could for them, then returned them to the wild and prayed they'd be all right and not taken advantage of by predators," Abraham said.

Abraham suddenly yawned. He wiped at his eyes with his long fingers. "I'm mighty tired and I haven't been in any fields to cause it," he said, then smiled softly over at Swift Horse. "I must admit, the long journey with such hurt to my back has taken much outta me. I hope I'll get my full strength back so that I can do my part 'round here. I look forward to my first hunt with your warriors."

"There is plenty of time for that," Swift Horse said, smiling at Abraham as he rose from the chair. He patted him on the shoulder. "I will go now. You and the fawn can go to bed. Tomorrow is another day. Perhaps you will be stronger then."

"I'm much happier, that's for sure," Abraham said, rising and holding the fawn near and dear to his heart. "Because of you, I'm happier. Thank you, Swift Horse. Thank you."

"I am happy to see that you are happy," Swift

Horse said, turning and walking toward the door. "I will see you tomorrow, Abraham. Get a good rest."

"I most certainly will," Abraham said, walking with Swift Horse to the door, closing it behind him after Swift Horse left.

Chapter 20

Love looks not with the eyes, but with the mind,
And therefore is wing'd Cupid painted blind.
—William Shakespeare

After having knocked more than once on Marsha's door, Swift Horse could not help but be concerned. Edward James hadn't said that she had gone anywhere. She should be home. He went to a window and peered inside.

What he saw made his heart skip a beat.

He saw Marsha's sewing equipment spilled along the floor beside a chair, and she wasn't anywhere in sight. And knowing how neat she was, having made Edward James's store "as neat as a pin," seeing her spilled sewing equipment and not seeing signs of her anywhere made a fear enter his heart that made Swift Horse feel ill.

He went back to the door. He tried it, but it was locked securely from the inside. That inspired hope, for if the door was locked, surely no intruders had come and caused Marsha some sort of trouble. Then he remembered the other door.

He knew that the door to the store wasn't always locked, for it was known wide and far by those who frequented the trading post that if anyone sneaked into the store for any reason, they could get shot on the spot.

Perhaps this time someone didn't heed that warning and went inside, especially if they knew that Edward James wasn't there to hold a rifle on them if they were caught there illegally.

Truly fearing for Marsha's safety now, he ran to the front door and found it agape.

Someone had stolen Marsha away!

"Marsha!" he cried as he rushed into the living quarters, stopping and staring again at the spilled sewing equipment. He turned and looked in jerks around him, stopping again at the spilled things.

"Someone did come and take her away," he growled, his teeth clenched, his hands in tight fists at his sides.

Breathing hard, and with a determination he had never felt before, he ran through the store, went outside, and fell to his knees and studied the footprints. He searched the ground and found footprints he knew were made only moments before, then stood tall and gazed, pondering, at his sister's cabin.

If he went and told Edward James about Marsha's disappearance, it would only slow things down, and he knew that time was wasting already, for he had no idea how long Marsha had been gone, or with whom.

He had to follow the tracks! And he would rather not have anyone with him to interfere in the search. The tracks soon led into the forest. It would be hard to follow them now, he knew, with the leaves such a cushion to anything or anybody who would be traveling over them. But all that he needed was the direction the person had taken after abducting Marsha, and he had it!

He hurried home, got his steed, and returned to the tracks that he had found.

He was puzzled, however, when he found another fresh pair, and he was taken aback when he noticed something different about those tracks. Someone had cleverly tied fur around the horse's hooves. He knew the trick and why it was used.

But this time it hadn't worked.

Swift Horse knew the art of tracking too well, and knew that more than one horse was involved in this abduction.

But the main thing was that he had a direction to go. He now suspected who was guilty of the crime. The direction of the tracks indicated to

Swift Horse that the cowkeeper had come and abducted Marsha.

Swift Horse was stunned that anyone would be this ignorant, or bold, to come right into the Creek village and steal the woman away who was soon to be the Creek chief's bride. How did he think he could hide her without being found?

"The stupidity of a white man, that's why," Swift Horse grumbled. He only hoped that that stupidity did not go further than the abduction itself, for if she was touched wrongly, sexually, or harmed in any way, ah, pity the man who did this to his woman!

With eyes alert as a cat's in the night, every bone in his body tight with anger, Swift Horse continued onward.

Chapter 21

So, either by the picture or my love,
Thyself away art present still with me.
—William Shakespeare

Marsha swallowed hard and licked her dry lips after the gag was removed from her mouth. But her wrists were still tied, and a rope had been wound around her to keep her tied in the chair that she had only moments ago been forced to sit on.

She was trying to be brave in the face of danger. Not only would her brother be out for blood, so would the entire Creek nation, for the cowkeeper had done a proud and powerful Creek chief's woman wrong.

She had no idea what to think, except that she knew that she was in mortal danger by a man who might suddenly realize what he had done and decide to do away with her in order to keep anyone from ever knowing that he had done such an asinine thing.

"This here room is going to be your home until I hear you tell me, with conviction, that you will cooperate with me," Alan Burton said.

"And what do I have to do . . . to . . . cooperate?" Marsha blurted out, trying not to show her fear. But she *was* so afraid that no one would ever find her. She had seen how the cowkeeper had to shove aside a heavy, huge chifforobe in order to get into this dark, windowless storage room.

Her heart sank, for she could not help but feel doomed at the hands of her abductor. And what he had in mind for her made her insides crawl. She knew that eventually he would force himself on her, sexually. She could see it in his pale and beady gray eyes that he had abducted her mainly for her, not as an act of vengeance against anyone.

He wanted her as his wife! He had told her that while riding toward his home.

"You make me want to vomit," she rushed out, defying him with an angry stare. "If you ever dare try to touch me, I shall fight you off by any means that I can."

"My beloved wife Sherry, God rest her soul, was a feisty one, too," Alan said, chuckling. "So don't try those type of threats on me. It only makes my loins get hotter."

Realizing that he was serious, and that she had just egged him on by saying the wrong things, Marsha said nothing else to him.

"Yep, golden-haired, pretty lady, in time you'll be tamed enough to be willing to do anything I say in order to get out of this dark, dank, and stinky room," Alan said. "You'll cooperate with me, all right. And when you do, I'll take you and my cows elsewhere so no one can ever find you. I'm tired of fighting with your brother and the Creek. I'm ready for some much-earned peace in my life and especially with a woman like you to share my bed each night."

"You're insane," Marsha said heatedly. "I'll never cooperate with you. Never!"

Alan shrugged. "If you're going to be that way, so be it," he said shrewdly. "I'll make your imprisonment worse than I originally planned. You'll not have food, heat, nor water for baths. You'll soon be willing to do anything in order to live a normal life again."

Smiling crookedly, he leaned down into her face. "You will even marry me," he said throatily.

Enraged more by the minute, Marsha spat at his feet.

Laughing menacingly, Alan walked from the

room and closed the door behind him, leaving Marsha in total darkness.

Tears filled Marsha's eyes as she tried to see around her in the dark, but it was pitch-black. Nothing was definable. All she knew was that she was a prisoner to a man who had gone to maddening lengths to have her.

"Please, oh please, Lord, let someone come and find me," she sobbed out into the darkness.

Chapter 22

Thou wast all that to me, love,
For which my soul did pine.
                    —Edgar Allan Poe

Feeling smug, Alan went to his liquor cabinet and pulled out a bottle of whiskey. Smiling, he opened it and poured himself one shot, and then another, and another, until he was beginning to feel drunk. He gazed at the chifforobe that he had scooted back in place. "The lady might want to drink with me," he said, his words drunkenly slurred.

He set the glass and the bottle of whiskey on a side table, then once again slid the chifforobe aside and opened the door.

Marsha's insides tightened when lamplight from the outer room poured into her prison. She trembled with fear when she saw the outline of Alan Burton standing in the doorway.

But she noticed something new about him.

He wasn't standing still. He was teetering, suddenly having to grab at the door frame to steady himself.

"You're . . . drunk . . ." she gasped, a new sort of fear grabbing at her heart with this knowledge.

"Perhaps I am, perhaps I ain't," Alan said, shrugging and chuckling.

He stepped back into the outer room again and grabbed the bottle of whiskey and the glass, then reentered the storage room. Enough light came through the door for him to see Marsha's face.

"You're mighty pretty, don'tcha know?" he said, his hands too full to be able to reach out and touch her. Instead, he leaned down into her face. "You're gonna make a mighty fine and pretty bride for this cowkeeper."

"There's nothing in hell you could do to make me accept marrying you," Marsha found the courage to say, yet gazing in fear at the whiskey, realizing how drunk Alan Burton already was.

He could hardly stand, and his speech was terribly slurred. She could smell his intoxication. His breath reeked of it as he stood now with his face so close to hers.

"You don't have a choice in the matter, Miss

Prissy," Alan said, then threw his head back in a fit of laughter.

"You are more insane than I first thought," Marsha said, her voice breaking. "How can you think you will get away with what you have done to me?"

"I don't think it, I know it," Alan said, again idly shrugging.

He straightened his back and tried to pour some whiskey into the glass, but laughed crookedly when he discovered that he got more on the sides of the glass than in it.

"Whoops," he said, trying again.

"Please leave me alone," Marsha asked, pleading with her eyes. "At least until you are sober . . ."

"If you'd drink with me, you'd think better of arguin' about what your future holds for you," Alan said, finally able to get enough whiskey in the glass.

He set the bottle on the floor, then stepped closer to Marsha.

He tipped the glass to her lips and began slowly feeding her the whiskey, Marsha gagging.

But soon her eyes were drawn quickly elsewhere.

Her heart skipped a beat when she saw a shadowy figure suddenly at the door, the light from the outer room illuminating it enough for her to see who it was!

Alan saw her eyes widening. He drew the glass slowly away.

"One Eye . . ." she gasped, knowing it was he even though he wasn't dressed as he did when he portrayed a man of peace. Tonight he wore war paint and a brief breechclout the same as he had on the day of the ambush.

But she knew without a doubt that it *was* One Eye. She recognized the same leer, the same stance . . . !

Hearing that name and seeing Marsha's alarm, Alan turned his head with a start. He froze when he saw the Indian painted in war paint, and with one eye, make a lunge toward him with a knife ready for its death plunge.

Alan turned and gave Marsha a terrified look just as One Eye sank the knife into his back.

One Eye watched Alan fall to the floor. He then kicked him aside and stood with his fists on his hips as he glared down at Marsha. "The cowkeeper getting drunk made my plan for you much more simple," One Eye said, laughing throatily.

He leaned closer to Marsha. "I had planned to kill both of you, but changed my mind," he said. He smiled wickedly at her. "That would be too simple . . . too quick. I want to make things more difficult and uncomfortable for you before killing you. You white witch, you almost caused my friend to believe you when you told him that I was the one-eyed man who killed your parents."

He threw his head back in a fit of laughter, then he looked soberly into Marsha's fearful eyes. "Little does my friend Swift Horse know, but I also killed his parents," he said tightly.

"No . . ." Marsha sobbed. "Oh, how can Swift Horse not see past your front of being a friend— of being an innocent man? He is so astute in everything else."

"We were young braves, learning ways of proud warriors together," One Eye said. "He will not allow himself to see that side of me that could never be as he wished me to be. I will never allow him to see it."

"What are you going to do with me?" Marsha asked warily, every bone in her body afraid.

"Enough has been said," One Eye said, reaching down and retrieving his knife from Alan's back. He wiped the blade clean on Alan's pants leg, then used it to slice the ropes away that held Marsha tied into the chair.

He quickly tied her wrists the minute she was freed of the chair, and then gagged her.

"I had planned to kill you immediately so that it would look like you and the cowkeeper killed each other, but I have other plans for you now," One Eye said, grabbing her by an arm and shoving her from the room.

When she looked over her shoulder at Alan Burton, who now lay in a pool of his own blood, Marsha became ill at her stomach. Then the true fear grabbed at her insides as One Eye led her out into the darkness of night and made her walk some distance before reaching a horse that he had left hidden amidst a thick forest of trees. He shoved her onto the horse and glared up at her, then mounted behind her. One Eye had recently bought the horse so he would have a steed that the Wind Clan would not recognize and trace back to him.

They rode through a tall stand of grass in hopes that his tracks would get lost in them, for he expected Swift Horse to be close behind. Once Marsha's absence was discovered at the village, Swift Horse would stop at nothing to find her.

That was the reason One Eye had not killed her immediately as he had originally planned. He wanted Swift Horse to search for her, knowing he would never find her. He would come across bones sometime in the future, and wonder if they might be the remains of the woman he loved.

He threw his head back in a fit of laughter, sending chills up and down Marsha's spine. She had thought she was in the company of a madman while she was with Alan Burton. His insanity was nothing compared to One Eye's!

Then a thought came to her. As she had given Alan Burton a last look, she only now remembered having seen him move just slightly. Could he still be alive? Could he tell everyone what she had been saying all along—that One Eye was the true culprit?

She prayed to herself that she was right, that he did have some life left in him. Strangely enough, that man, the cowkeeper—who had abducted her, whom she abhorred—was possibly now her only hope!

Chapter 23

Just as Swift Horse had expected, the tracks led to the cowkeeper's ranch house. He stayed in the shadows of the trees, his gaze sweeping the area.

Seeing lamplight in several of Alan's windows made Swift Horse know that from this point on, he must be more careful, especially if he was going to catch the evil man in the act of keeping Swift Horse's woman hostage.

Swift Horse couldn't believe that the cowkeeper could be so daft as to steal a woman right beneath Swift Horse's nose and think he would get away with it! Tonight the man would know just how wrong he was. He would also know the wrath of a Creek chief who had been wronged now in the worst way possible, by his taking the chief's woman as his captive!

He dismounted, tethered his reins to a low tree limb, then yanked his knife from the sheath at his right side. His eyes narrowed angrily, he moved stealthily and quickly through the darkness until he reached the house. Swift Horse hugged the wall of the ranch house with his back as he inched closer to a window with lamplight spilling from it.

His heart thumping wildly in hopes of having his woman with him again in only a matter of moments, Swift Horse stepped around so that he could see through the window.

Not seeing anything amiss in this room, and not seeing any signs of the cowkeeper, Swift Horse moved quickly to the door, quietly opened it, then stepped inside.

Silence met him there.

He stayed there for a moment longer, his eyes scanning the room again, and then gazed at doors, two of which led into two different directions from the room.

He chose one of them and hurried to it, stopping and staring when he saw another door at the end of this room that stood open, a huge piece of furniture having been shoved aside.

Puzzled now by what he had found, and sensing something was very wrong, Swift Horse inched across the room. When he reached the open door, he stopped and gazed intently into the storage room.

He took a quick step back when he saw someone just inside the door, sprawled on the floor on his stomach, blood on his back.

"Cowkeeper," Swift Horse said, then hurried into the dark room and knelt down on a knee beside Alan Burton. He placed a finger to the man's throat and felt a faint pulse beat. Just as he drew his finger away, he saw the cowkeeper's eyes flutter slowly open.

"One . . . Eye . . . Marsha," he managed to say in a strangled sort of whisper as he looked wild-eyed at Swift Horse.

"What?" Swift Horse gasped, his eyebrows forking. "You said one eye, and then Marsha. Do you mean that the one-eyed man was here? He did this to you? He took my woman?"

Alan gave him a strange sort of stare, then his body lurched, his arms tightened at his sides, and he gasped out his last breath of life.

"Cowkeeper," Swift Horse said, turning him on his back. "Cowkeeper!"

But Alan didn't reply. His eyes were locked in a death's stare, a tear having run from the corner of one of them.

"You *did* steal my woman away, and now someone else has her," Swift Horse said tightly.

His gaze looked slowly around the room, his throat somewhat constricting when he saw the ropes that had fallen from the chair. He could only guess that was where the cowkeeper had placed Marsha upon their arrival here. He had tied her to the chair, and then someone else came and released her and was now taking her . . . *where*?

"He said one eye, and then . . . Marsha," Swift Horse said, so wishing that he knew how to interpret that.

Did he mean that a one-eyed man was there? Or did he mean that the man who was there was . . . One Eye?

He sighed heavily as he respectfully closed Alan's eyes although this man had done him and his woman so wrong. But Swift Horse was a religious man, who understood what it meant to respect the dead—even the death of someone he loathed.

He reached for a blanket and placed it over Alan Burton, then hurried from the room and ran outside.

He mounted his horse and rode out into the open. He studied the track activity all around the house, then followed what he found until he came to a tall stand of grass that reached out far and wide in all directions.

The one who had taken Marsha knew that it would be difficult to follow them in such tall and weaving grass. Swift Horse had to think like the one he was tracking and choose a direction, hoping that he would eventually be led to his woman.

Hopefully she would still be alive!

He snapped his reins hard, sank his heels into the flanks of his steed, and took off at a hard gallop.

Chapter 24

Those hours, that with gentle work did frame
The lovely gaze where every eye doth dwell. . . .
—William Shakespeare

One Eye looked down at Marsha where he held her on his lap on his horse. He could see pleading in her eyes and he could hear her trying to say something behind the gag.

For now he ignored her. He just smiled and continued onward, too full of himself and what he had achieved tonight not to feel proud and smug.

He was on his way to his hideout, and would then decide exactly what he would do with Marsha. It just didn't seem enough for him to kill her outright. There needed to be more than that for him to feel that he had made her pay for having interfered in his life—a double life that combined the excitement of being a chief with the notoriety of being a renegade.

Yes, soon he would think up a way to make this lady pay, and in the worst way possible. But until then, he had to get her out of the area, so that none of Swift Horse's warriors could find her—*that* would come later!

He smiled darkly at knowing that he had taken the lady away from Swift Horse—to whom everything came so easily. Swift Horse had always been the one everyone looked up to over One Eye.

Even One Eye's own clan admired Swift Horse more than they should when they had their own leader. It was just that Swift Horse had always had more of a noble bearing about him than One Eye.

He gazed at Marsha, who was still making all sorts of noises behind her gag, her eyes pleaded with him in the moonlight.

"All right, what is it?" he said, yanking the gag from around her mouth, yet holding tightly to it, for he planned to keep her gagged until they were safely at his well-concealed hideout, which no one yet had been able to find even though many soldiers had scanned the land for him and his gang.

"I'm so thirsty," Marsha said. "Please give me a drink of water."

Needing a drink as well, and a moment or two

to stretch from having been in the saddle for so long, One Eye didn't hesitate doing as she requested. He rode onward as he watched for the shine of water beneath the moonlight, knowing that he was near Silver Creek, where he had stopped ofttimes to refresh himself.

"Please, One Eye, I am so parched," Marsha pleaded, thinking that he was ignoring her.

She kept glancing at the gag that he was still holding, expecting him to stop and place it back on her at any moment. She hoped that he would leave it off long enough for her to be able to cry out with alarm if they came anywhere near a settler's home, or if by chance someone came along on a horse.

Yet she reminded herself what time of night it was. It was surely the midnight hour now, for it seemed an eternity since she had been sitting peacefully beside the fire, crocheting. Now she doubted she had many more hours to live.

Oh, if only Swift Horse would have listened to her when she had told him that One Eye was the villain! Even her brother had scoffed at the idea. She hoped it wouldn't be too late when they discovered that she was right.

She gazed heavenward at the many twinkling stars, and prayed to herself that soon this nightmare would end. Her brother never went to bed late. As far back as she could remember he got sleepy long before she. Surely he had discovered that she was missing by now and had alarmed Swift Horse. Together they would find her. Finally One Eye would get his comeuppance.

"You asked for water, you have water," One Eye said, drawing Marsha from her deep, troubled thoughts.

She gazed to the right as One Eye turned his horse in that direction. She smiled to herself and said a quiet prayer of thanks to the heavens when she saw the shine of water not that far away. It was one of the many creeks that dissected this land, where water was always refreshing and cold.

She tried the ropes at her wrists again, knowing that she had succeeded at getting them loose. Perhaps soon . . . ! And then she would find a way to disable One Eye and make her own escape without anyone's help.

She was determined that this man wasn't going to take her life, too, after having taken her parents' lives as well as those of Swift Horse's parents.

She would proudly take One Eye—dead—to Swift Horse, and once and for all prove to him that she had been right about his best friend.

One Eye reined in his black steed and dismounted, then reached up and took Marsha from the saddle.

"Thank you so much," she murmured, pretending to be gracious. If at all possible, and if she got the courage, she was going to kill this man—a villain of villains.

She tried the ropes again, her heart thudding hard inside her chest when she discovered that now all she had to do was slide her hands free!

"Come with me," One Eye said, nodding toward the creek as he began walking toward it, seeing that Marsha was staying directly at his side. "But hurry. I want to get you into hiding before daybreak."

"We have that much farther to go?" Marsha asked, now playing along with him, knowing that true freedom was only a few heartbeats away if everything went as planned.

She eyed his knife.

It was at his left side, the side on which she was walking.

She could grab it in an instant.

But no, she quickly thought. No matter how much she hated this man, she couldn't kill him with a knife. She couldn't even think about how it must feel to sink a knife into another person's flesh. No. There had to be a better way.

She stepped up to the water with One Eye.

Suddenly he gave her a shove that made her fall quickly to the ground on her knees, causing pain to shoot through them—and her ropes to fall away.

But One Eye hadn't noticed.

An owl hooting suddenly in a tree above them startled him.

Marsha could tell that he was troubled by the owl, for he had gasped and searched the tree limbs above him for the night bird. Marsha realized why he was reacting to the owl in such a way. She had studied Indian lore while she was in school in Georgia, and had read that owls frightened some Indians, who took their presence for a bad omen.

Marsha's heart pounded as she realized this was her opportunity to act, and act quickly.

One Eye still hadn't noticed that her wrists were free. His back was to her as he continued to look for the owl that had repeated its call into the night, this time seeming to be closer, almost straight above her on the low-hanging limbs of a willow tree.

Forgetting how her knees ached from the hard fall and thinking only one thing now—escape—Marsha moved to her feet. Her eyes searched around her, then stopped when she saw a large rock. It wasn't too large for her to pick up, yet large enough to hopefully crack open this evil man's skull.

Breathing hard and knowing that every second counted now, she picked up the rock and stepped quickly behind him. Just as he started to turn, she lowered the rock to his head, hitting him on the left of his skull.

The sound when she hit him was like a walnut cracking. Marsha felt suddenly ill at her stomach, especially when she saw blood pouring from the head wound as One Eye crumpled to the ground, silent and still.

Marsha stared down at him. She had gotten the best of a man whom surely no one had ever bested!

And . . . and he did seem dead, but she was still afraid to get too close to him, to check for a pulse beat in the vein of his throat, because he might be conscious enough to grab her and kill her with his knife. Marsha decided to leave well enough alone.

She could return home! She could bring her brother and Swift Horse back there, so they could witness for themselves, once and for all, that she had not been imagining things when she had said that One Eye was the horrible one-eyed killer!

She ran to the horse, her knees suddenly rubbery and weak from the ordeal she had just been through, but managed to get in the saddle. She grabbed the reins, took one last look at One Eye, then wheeled the horse around and headed, hopefully, back in the direction of the Creek village. However, she soon realized that she wasn't sure at all where she was. She was confused in the dark. Everywhere she looked things seemed the same, and if she rode in a circle, she might end up back where she had left One Eye.

She studied the stars, then the moon, and then the lay of the land. She still didn't know which way to go. She was lost!

Near to tears, Marsha snapped the reins and prayed that she would somehow find the right way home. Then something worse sent a cold fear through her. It was the sound of an approaching horse! What if it was someone from One Eye's renegade gang?

"Oh, please, no . . ." she sobbed, panic filling her very being.

She looked to the right.

She looked to the left.

When she found thick brush and trees at her right side, she rode hurriedly toward them. She dismounted and clung to the reins to wait for the stranger to ride past. Then she would resume her own journey into the night and hope that the good Lord above would guide her in the right direction.

The horse was now so close she could hear its heaving as it rode hard in the night. Marsha stared through the brush so that she might be able to see the rider's face.

If it was a renegade, she would soon know.

It was as though a breath of fresh air had suddenly been blown onto Marsha's face when she saw just who it was! "Swift Horse!" she cried, running out into his horse's path.

Swift Horse could hardly believe his eyes. There his woman stood, waving him down . . . unharmed!

He drew a tight rein, causing his horse to stop abruptly. He still couldn't believe his eyes. He had prayed to the Supreme God in the Heavens, the Master of Breath, that he would find Marsha—and not injured in any way—and his prayer had been answered.

There his woman was, and she wasn't injured! Not in any way that was visible to him, at least.

He knew that the trauma of the situation had surely caused her much inward pain. He would kiss it away!

He leaped from his horse and grabbed Marsha into his arms. He held her tightly, aware of how much she was trembling and clinging to him.

"It was One Eye!" she cried. "He . . . he . . . abducted me." She eased from his arms and gazed up into his eyes, the moon still high and bright above them.

"But I was first taken by the cowkeeper," she said, still finding it incredible that Swift Horse was there, and that she was going to be all right!

"I know," Swift Horse said, his arms still around her waist, his eyes devouring her. "I followed the tracks to the cowkeeper's house. I went inside. I found him."

"One Eye killed him," Marsha gulped out, recalling the viciousness of the attack with the knife.

"He lived long enough to say three words," Swift Horse said softly. "He said one, eye, and Marsha."

"Then you know!" Marsha cried. "You finally know that the one-eyed man was One Eye!"

"The cowkeeper did not identify the man specifically," Swift Horse said thickly. "He said one eye, not that it was One Eye."

"Are you saying that you still don't believe it was One Eye?" Marsha said, finding it hard not to shout at him. How could he *not* believe that it was One Eye? How could she ever make him believe it if he did not believe it now?

"I still cannot see my friend as a renegade,"

Swift Horse said. "Was this man dressed as a renegade—or as One Eye dresses?"

"As . . ." Marsha gulped out: "He wore a breechclout and war paint on his face."

"Then do you not see?" Swift Horse said, so wanting to believe that his friend could not have done this thing. "One Eye has never worn a breechclout or the paint of a renegade."

"Of course he wouldn't in front of you," Marsha cried, getting more frustrated by the minute. "Or anyone else he wanted to fool."

She hung her head, then gazed into Swift Horse's eyes. "It was all so horrible," she sobbed. "Alan Burton abducted me from my home then locked me in a room with no windows. He kept the door hidden behind a chifforobe. He had it slid aside and was forcing whiskey on me when One Eye arrived. After One Eye plunged the knife into Alan Burton's back, he took me. I'm not sure what his final plans were for me."

Swift Horse slowly shook his head back and forth. "I still cannot accept that One Eye is the one who did this to you," he said tightly, then his eyes widened. "Marsha, how did you escape?"

She quickly explained how it had happened.

"I'm not sure if he is dead or alive," she gulped out. "I was afraid to get close enough to check his pulse. I was so afraid that he'd grab me and kill me before he died himself."

"Can you remember where you left the man?" Swift Horse asked, searching her eyes.

"I'm so lost," she cried. "I'm not sure of anything." Then she said, "But we can't be that far from where I left him, because I haven't been traveling for all that long."

"The horse's tracks from where you left the one-eyed man will lead us back to him," Swift Horse said. "Come. We shall follow them. We will find him."

Marsha silently prayed that One Eye would still be there. Finally Swift Horse would know he was the one-eyed man. Finally the proof would be there, staring him in the face.

Marsha got One Eye's horse. She walked beside Swift Horse as his eyes stayed glued to the ground as he walked his own steed, following the tracks. They wandered onward, and then Marsha grabbed at Swift Horse's arm.

"The creek," she said tightly. "Over there. That's where you will find him."

"There are many creeks . . ." Swift Horse said, gazing into her eyes.

"I know, but I'm almost certain this is where it happened," she murmured, the sound of the owl still making its eerie night call convincing her.

They walked onward, then Marsha stopped and stared blankly where she had left One Eye, the bloody rock proving that this was absolutely where she had left him—but he was gone!

"He's still alive," she gasped out, paling at the very thought of him still out there ready to wreak more havoc, and surely more eager to kill her now than before. She, a woman, had bested him.

She looked desperately at Swift Horse. "He's alive—and gone," she said, her voice drawn.

"For now it is enough that you are alive and well," he said quickly, grabbing Marsha against him, holding her tightly. "My woman, had that man killed you . . ."

"I'm fine," she softly explained.

Their lips came together in a quivering, warm and sweet kiss, but Marsha could not keep her mind on the kiss or embrace. She could not help but fear One Eye's escape.

Oh, Lord . . . where was he?

Chapter 25

That was all I meant,
—To be just
And the passion I had raised,
To content.
                    —Robert Browning

Edward James stood staring at Marsha's sewing basket. "Where is Marsha?" he said thickly, not certain now what to do. When he had arrived home and found her sewing equipment spilled at the foot of the chair where she always sat and sewed before the fire, panic had grabbed at his gut.

His sister was too particular to have left her thread and sewing needles on the floor. They were there because someone had come in after he had left his sister to visit Soft Wind.

Someone had abducted her!

He had hurried to Swift Horse's cabin to seek his help, or to see if, just by chance, Marsha was there. Perhaps Swift Horse had discovered her missing, as well, and had gone and found her.

But when Edward James had found no one at Swift Horse's cabin and had seen that his favorite steed was gone, he could only assume that Swift Horse was out there searching for Marsha and the man who abducted her.

Edward James began pacing, then stopped and lifted a log onto the fire. He turned and gazed at the back door. He knew Marsha had double-bolted it. That had to mean that whoever came uninvited came through his store.

He doubled a fist and raised it in the air. "How could I be so foolish to think no one would come into my store at night?" he shouted, his face hot with anger. "Threats mean nothing to those who have an agenda. Tonight that agenda was my sister!"

He thought about who might have taken her and came up with two prospects.

The cowkeeper, who had come to claim his reward after saving her from the fire.

And then there was the one-eyed man who might have heard that she was hell-bent on finding him and making him pay for his crimes.

"And what if that one-eyed man *is* One Eye?" he whispered harshly, lowering his hand to his side.

He shuddered at the thought of that possibility, and remembered how he had ignored his sister when she had said that he was the one who had murdered their parents. If One Eye *was* the culprit, he could be the one to have done this asinine deed tonight, to silence her.

"Please let nothing happen to her," Edward James said as he gazed upward, seeking help from the Almighty. "Please, oh please, let Swift Horse find her—find her untouched."

The sound of an arriving horse outside his cabin made his throat suddenly constrict.

His heart thumped wildly inside his chest from fear of possibly being moments away from discovering that something terrible might have happened to his beloved sister. If so, he wasn't sure if he would want to live, either.

His knees almost rubbery from fear, Edward James went to the back door and hurried outside. He felt keen relief rush through him when he found not only Swift Horse there, but also his sister.

"What happened?" Edward James asked, his voice drawn as he hurried up to them, eager to take his sister in his arms. "Sis, where . . . who . . . ?"

Understanding how anxious her brother was for answers, Marsha stepped away from Swift Horse and flung herself into her big brother's arms.

"I'm all right," she murmured as he held her tightly against him, tears streaming from his eyes.

She gazed up at him. "Big brother, you're crying," she said, stepping away from him. She reached a finger to his face and wiped away the tears. "I'm so sorry I had you this frightened, but . . . but . . . I had no control over what the men did," she said, her voice breaking.

"Men?" Edward James gasped, his eyes widening. "Lord, sis, what men? And what did they do to you?"

"Edward James, I am not harmed in any way, especially not the way you might be thinking," Marsha murmured. "Let's go inside. I'm bone-weary from the experience. I'd like to sit down. And then I'll tell you everything."

Swift Horse stepped up to them. He took one of her hands. "I will leave you now," he said, looking slowly from Marsha to Edward James. "You can talk, and I have someone to see."

"You have someone to see this late at night?" Marsha asked, searching his eyes.

"I must consult my shaman about what has happened and seek his help to find the one-eyed man," he said, his jaw tight.

He tried not to envision that that one-eyed man might be his friend One Eye, even though

Marsha still tried to convince him that he was. He could not see how One Eye could ever be his enemy, when they had been soul mates—best friends—for so long.

"The one-eyed man?" Edward James gasped. He looked quickly at Marsha. "He did this . . . ?"

Marsha nodded. "Yes, he is the very one, the same man who has torn so many lives apart," she murmured.

She turned to Swift Horse. "One day you will believe me when I tell you that the one-eyed man is One Eye, your friend—who is, in truth, your worst enemy," she said, her voice drawn. "He is playing a good game, still, of being your friend, but truly is evil through and through."

"I want to believe you, too, because you wouldn't want to turn me against someone I have loved as a friend for so long," Swift Horse said, frowning.

He swallowed hard. "In time, everyone will know the man's true identity, and he will pay for his crimes. If he is One Eye, he will also pay for having played games with this Creek's heart," Swift Horse said emotionally.

"One day you will see that I am right about this man," Marsha murmured. "A lot of people aren't who they seem to be, or want people to believe they are."

She leaned into his embrace and gave him a comforting hug. "I understand how you can't accept what I say as fact," she murmured. "But in time, it will be proved to you. I'm just so sorry that when you do discover the truth, the hurt will be harder, for the longer he gets away with tricking you, the more it will humiliate and hurt you once the truth is known about him."

Marsha swallowed hard, for she hated thinking about the day when he would be faced with the truth. That truth would cut like a knife into his heart, a heart that had trusted this one-eyed man for far too long.

She stepped away from Swift Horse as he mounted his horse. "Swift Horse, thank you for coming and finding me," Marsha murmured, tears stinging at the corners of her eyes—tears of happiness for being alive.

Swift Horse gave her a smile that made her insides melt, then rode off in the direction of Bright Moon's cabin. Marsha understood his need to be with Bright Moon.

"Come on, sis," Edward James said, taking her by a hand. "I want to hear it all. You mentioned the one-eyed man. Who was the other man?" He stopped and gazed at her. "Or do I even need ask?"

"I'm sure you are assuming right," Marsha

murmured. "The man who came for me and abducted me first was Alan Burton."

"Alan Burton, the cowkeeper . . ." Edward James said between clenched teeth. "I had thought he might be the one."

"I'll tell you all about it," Marsha said, reaching a comforting hand to his cheek. "Let's go in and sit by the fire. It is just so good to be home."

"Home?" Edward James said, slowly smiling. "That is the first time you referred to my home as yours."

"I know," Marsha said, walking into the lamplit room. "I have never let myself adjust. There was always the one-eyed man getting in the way of seeing this home as mine. Because of him, we no longer have a mother and father to be a part of that home. But now? At this moment, Edward James, you make me feel as though I have just come home."

He turned and hugged her, then closed and locked the door behind them.

He took her hand and led her over to a rocking chair and sat down beside her.

"First I want you to know that the store door is locked and it will be from now on when I am not in the store during working hours," Edward James said. "I trusted too much, but living here among the Creek, I didn't see anyone being brazen enough to break into my store. I see that I was wrong. I have trusted too easily."

"You have such a good heart, that is why you trust so easily," Marsha said. She ran her fingers through her thick golden hair, combing out the tangles caused by her times on the horses tonight.

Edward James leaned forward and clasped his hands together. "Tell me from the beginning," he said. "Tell me everything."

"I shall," Marsha replied. She settled back in the rocking chair, tired and needing the comfort of her bed, yet knew that she must tell Edward James everything first.

She began with how she had been there enjoying sewing, and how she had heard a noise in the outer room, thinking it was him coming back for something. But, instead, it had been . . .

"Alan Burton," she said, shivering at the thought of how she had been treated by him. Then she told him everything up to the point that she had seen Swift Horse and how wonderful it had been that he had seemed to come out of the blue and rescued her.

"You actually rendered the one-eyed man unconscious?" Edward James said, chuckling. "My little sister who cringes when she has to even

swat a fly—you knocked a man unconscious
with a rock?"

"Edward James, I rendered One Eye unconscious, not just a nameless one-eyed man," Marsha said, then sighed. "One day everyone will
believe me. It has to happen. This man is getting
clumsy and careless and not using the best of
judgment about things."

Marsha nodded. "Yes, it is One Eye, even
though you still don't believe me," she murmured. "And actually, Edward James, I had
hoped worse for him than just being unconscious. I was afraid that if I didn't kill him, I'd be
doomed."

"And then he escaped anyway," Edward
James said, scowling. His jaw tightened. "He
won't get away with this. He won't have enough
places to hide. He'll be found and dealt with."

"He doesn't need to hide because no one be-
lieves he is who he is," Marsha said dryly. "But
when everyone does finally believe me, I will
feel sorry for One Eye's people, his Wolf Clan of
Creek," Marsha murmured. "He's their chief.
They looked up to him. They see him as some
sort of hero."

Edward James listened, but didn't say anything. Inside his heart, he was beginning to believe his sister.

"Edward James, One Eye plays the role of being a kind, generous man, a leader of his people, to the fullest, while in truth, he is a demon," Marsha murmured. "But his time is almost over. I'll see to that."

"You look so tired," Edward James said, rising from his chair. He reached a hand out for Marsha.

She placed her hand in his and rose from her own chair. They embraced, then Edward James walked her to her bedroom.

He embraced her one last time, then walked to his bedroom as Marsha closed the door behind her and sighed as she looked around slowly. For a time tonight she thought she would never see this room—or civilization as she always had known it—again.

She went to the window and saw that the moon was no longer in the sky.

Instead soft, pinkish hues were being reflected along the horizon from the first breath of morning that was suddenly there.

"Thank the Lord, I *am* home," she whispered, sighing heavily.

Chapter 26

Let a man contend to the uttermost
For his life's set prize, be it what it will!
———Robert Browning

The morning was soft and pretty when Swift Horse went to Bright Moon's cabin and spoke his name outside the door. He knew his shaman's habits very well, and he knew that he was always awake with the birds, preparing himself for his full day of meetings with anyone who might need his guidance.

This morning his chief needed guidance, for Swift Horse's heart was heavy. He was beginning to believe now that the warrior who had been his friend for so long might not be at all who he had professed to be. Swift Horse could not believe that Marsha could be this mistaken.

"My chief, do come in," Bright Moon said as he opened the door for Swift Horse, his long gray hair coiled around his head, a robe of fur warming his old body.

Bright Moon stepped aside, his brow furrowing into a questioning frown when he saw the troubled look on Swift Horse's face.

Swift Horse sat down on a pallet of blankets on the floor in front of the fire and Bright Moon sat beside him.

"Tell me what is troubling you," Bright Moon said, placing a hand on one of Swift Horse's.

"It is something hard to say," Swift Horse said. He gave Bright Moon a troubled frown. "I am not certain, even, if I can."

"You have not slept the full night," Bright Moon said, studying Swift Horse's weary eyes. "Why is that, my chief? What kept you from your bed?"

"You do not know?" Swift Horse said, searching his shaman's pale brown eyes. Then he shook his head. "No. You would not know for I did not share what I was doing with anyone. Edward James's sister was abducted tonight."

"Marsha was abducted?" Bright Moon gasped, drawing his hand quickly away from Swift Horse. "Is she still missing?"

"No, she is safely home with her brother now. I found her and brought her home," Swift Horse said, somewhat tightly. "But the fact that she was abducted lies heavy on my heart. I was not there to protect her. And she had to suffer at the hands of two men tonight, not one."

"Two . . . ?" Bright Moon asked, his eyes widening. "Tell me about it, Swift Horse."

"When I went to her cabin and saw that she was gone and that her sewing equipment was strewn across the floor, I knew that something had to have happened to her," Swift Horse said thickly. "I went outside. I followed tracks to the cowkeeper's house."

"The cowkeeper?" Bright Moon said, leaning forward and gazing more intensely into Swift Horse's eyes. "He did this?"

"He was the first," Swift Horse said.

"The first?" Bright Moon asked, finding this more and more incredulous by the moment.

"He abducted Marsha from her home, and then the one-eyed renegade went there and killed Alan Burton and took Marsha with him," Swift Horse said, now almost hoarsely, he was so troubled, still, by what had happened to his woman.

"You say . . . a one-eyed man?" Bright Moon said, his voice drawn. "The same who killed your parents, others of our village, and various white settlers who come to our land or pass through it?"

"It must be the same, and I need your guidance about what I am thinking now," Swift Horse said, sighing heavily.

"What are you thinking?" Bright Moon asked.

When Swift Horse didn't answer right away, Bright Moon reached over and gently patted him on a knee. "I see it is hard for you to say," he said softly. "I urge you, though, to say it aloud instead of keeping it locked up inside your heart."

"If I am right about what I am thinking, I doubt I shall ever be able to fully accept it, for it is something that will tear at my very being if it is true," Swift Horse said stiffly. He reached up and pushed his heavy hair back from his shoulders, then again rested his hands on his knees. "But I know it is best to say it, not continue to just think it."

"And that is why you came to your shaman this hour of morning, is it not?" Bright Moon said, placing his own hands now on his own knees.

"Yes, I need to say it and then know what your feelings are about it," Swift Horse said, turning to gaze into his shaman's old eyes once again. "Bright Moon, my woman has said more than once that the one-eyed man is One Eye. She saw him murder her parents and says that is why she can never forget him. This man's face is in her mind's eye, always. How can she be this wrong? And, Bright Moon, how *can* there be two men with the exact scarrings of One Eye?"

"She does believe it is he?" Bright Moon said softly.

"None other," Swift Horse said, inhaling a deep, nervous breath. "I cannot continue to openly doubt her. She is taking offense, and I want no ill feelings between us. If she is so absolutely certain this man is One Eye, how can I continue to ignore this? He might be guilty of many crimes."

"Your best friend, who has always professed to be our clan's ally, might, instead, be our most ardent enemy?" Bright Moon said, now slowly shaking his head back and forth. "If that is so . . ."

"If that is so, I must stop him," Swift Horse rushed out. "I cannot allow him to put on a false face of friendship when, in truth, he might be the worst sort of man on this earth."

"And so you are truly believing now that One Eye *is* the one-eyed man," Bright Moon said, searching Swift Horse's eyes. "I see it in your eyes . . . I hear it in your voice . . . the hurt, the humiliation . . . the anger."

"Yes, I feel all of those things," Swift Horse

said. He placed a hand on Bright Moon's shoulder. "Will you help me?"

"My chief, I have always been here for you, as I was here for your father and grandfather before you," Bright Moon said, nodding. "Tell me. What would you ask of me?"

"I would like for you to make medicine that will harm the man who is guilty of crimes we have spoken of today," Swift Horse said. "If word is brought to me that One Eye is ill, then I will know for certain that he is the one who should pay for the crimes committed by the one-eyed man."

"His injury?" inquired Bright Moon.

"The one-eyed man who killed the cowkeeper and then abducted Marsha is carrying around a head injury today, for Marsha hit him over the head with a stone. She knocked him unconscious. I saw blood on the ground caused by the injury. This has to mean that if One Eye is the one who did this thing, he will not be able to hide the injury left by the blow."

"That should be enough proof, do you not think, without my making medicines that will harm him more than he is already harmed?" Bright Moon asked softly.

"Yes, that *is* enough," Swift Horse said, nodding.

"You will go to his village today and ask for him and see whether or not he is the injured one?" Bright Moon asked, bringing his robe more snugly around him. "To see if he is friend or foe?"

"No," Swift Horse said tightly. "It is better that I wait for him to come to me. You know that not too many days have ever passed when we have not met and talked. I am anxious to know whether or not he is truly the enemy, yet a part of me says to wait."

"It is because you are *afraid* to know?" Bright Moon said, reaching again and patting Swift Horse's knee. "The longer you go without knowing, the longer you can still feel a friendship you are fighting against losing."

"Yes, that is somewhat true," Swift Horse said, nodding. "But when I truly know for certain that he is the one who has left a bloody trail behind him, I will not hesitate to make him pay."

"When will you allow yourself to know . . . to accept?" Bright Moon asked.

"Our two clans are supposed to come together soon for the Busk Ceremony, so I shall wait and see if he comes, or stays at his home, which would prove he is hiding something—namely another scar that will never go away," Swift Horse said, slowly rising. "I have waited this long to know the truth, I can wait awhile longer. I would like for him to feel that he got away with this latest evil deed, and then allow him to step directly into a trap."

"You do speak as though you now truly believe he is the one-eyed man," Bright Moon said, also rising and walking Swift Horse to the door.

"Yes," Swift Horse said, turning and hugging Bright Moon.

"Will the woman be in danger the longer the one-eyed man is allowed to be free?" Bright Moon asked as he returned the hug.

"No one will ever get close enough to harm her ever again," Swift Horse said, stepping away from Bright Moon. "She will be guarded."

He went outside, and Bright Moon came with him.

Swift Horse looked up at the sky, then over at Marsha's cabin, and then at Bright Moon. "My woman was weary from her trying ordeal," he said. "She will be asleep for some time today. This will give me time to do something else that must be done."

"And that is?" Bright Moon asked as he walked Swift Horse to his mount.

"I have never cared for the cowkeeper, but it is not a good thing to leave his death unreported," he said as he started to swing himself into his saddle, but stopped when he saw Edward James step into the doorway of his store, waving at him.

"I am going to Fort Hill to tell Colonel Harris about Alan Burton's death so that the soldiers can collect his body and give him a proper burial," he said.

"And what of his cows and other animals?" Bright Moon asked.

"I am certain the soldiers will take them away," Swift Horse said, gazing at Edward James as he walked toward them.

"It is certain that the cows will not be in our corn ever again," Bright Moon said.

"Nor will the man be a problem again for our people, especially Marsha," Swift Horse said. "Had I seen the true evil in the man, I would have known that he could do something as underhanded as to steal my woman away."

"That is behind you now," Bright Moon said. "But you have something else to work through. Go now, and I will pray for this that is troubling you."

"Thank you," Swift Horse said, smiling at Edward James, who walked briskly up to him and stopped.

"Your sister still sleeps?" Swift Horse asked, placing a hand on Edward James's shoulder.

"Very soundly—and the back door is locked and we can see the front door," Edward James said. He looked at Swift Horse and then at Bright Moon. "After last night, I was made aware of how quickly things can change and how quickly a loved one can be gone from one's life."

Edward James paused, then said, "I want to marry your sister today, Swift Horse. If she doesn't feel strong enough for the formal ceremony, then we can exchange vows as she lies in her bed."

"I *am* strong enough, Edward James."

Edward James turned with a start. He gazed in wonder at Soft Wind, who was walking toward him, then slid his arms around her waist when she stepped up to him. "You are out of bed," he said, smiling. "You are much better."

"I am well enough to become your wife," Soft Moon said. "And I want to marry you today, too. We should not delay it another day." She looked at her brother and Bright Moon. "Can we?" she asked. "Or will it be too much trouble to do this so quickly?"

"Nothing I ever do for you is any trouble," Swift Horse said, seeing the tears of joy that this brought to his sister's eyes. He took her from Edward James, drawing her into his gentle embrace. "After the noon hour," he said, smiling

into her eyes. "I must leave to take care of business, but when I return I will see that my sister
becomes a wife to my friend Edward James."

Then he stepped away from her and stepped
up to Edward James. "Keep an eye on your sister
while I am gone," he warned. "I will double the
sentries around my village."

"No one will ever be able to harm my sister
again," Edward James said tightly as Soft Moon
eased to his side, his arm sliding around her
waist and holding her next to him.

"I will return in time for your wedding," Swift
Horse said, then swung himself into his saddle
and rode away.

Chapter 27

Some silent laws our hearts will make,
Which they shall long obey.
—William Wordsworth

A miracle seemed to have touched Soft Wind, for today, the day of her marriage, she had gotten up from her bed after a peaceful night of sleep and felt completely well! The scar from the terrible accident was now only a pucker of skin, and she was almost as strong as before the day the arrow had slammed into her shoulder.

Marsha gazed at her as she stood with Edward James, the two exchanging wondrous words as Bright Moon presided over the special event. The marriage ceremony was all but over and soon would come much merriment.

Marsha could not help but feel the excitement building inside her heart knowing that soon she and Swift Horse would be exchanging vows, too.

She had secretly hoped that they could speak theirs along with Edward James and Soft Wind.

But there was not enough time for Marsha and Swift Horse to ready themselves for their own nuptials, and it seemed that it was only right that this was Edward James and Soft Wind's day.

As Bright Moon was now speaking of the Supreme God in the Heavens, who was the Master of Breath, to her brother and Soft Wind, Marsha looked slowly around her. She had not known about this huge rotunda, which was used for ceremonial functions such as weddings, diplomatic negotiations, and assemblies of various kinds, particularly special meetings between Creek clans. It was larger than the council house that sat in the center of the village.

This was a circular building, thirty feet in diameter and made of logs. A low tunnel entranceway led into the council chamber, and seats lined the walls all around the circular room. More seats were positioned a few feet away in the same sort of circle, leaving room for people to walk between them.

The seats were filled now with people of only the Wind Clan, the ceremony having been decided upon too quickly to send invitations around to others.

Marsha was disappointed for only one reason.

She had hoped to see how One Eye reacted to his invitation—whether he would have come or not. She had not expected him to, for the wound to his head would prove that he was the one who accosted her and who had spread death and destruction everywhere.

She was trying terribly hard to understand why Swift Horse had not yet gone and spoken with One Eye. She assumed it was because he was afraid of what he would uncover—that just perhaps he could not handle the truth.

She shifted her thoughts back to where she was now, and why.

"You seem restless," Swift Horse whispered as he leaned closer to her.

"I'm sorry," she whispered back, taken by how handsome he was today. He wore a full outfit of fringed buckskin, heavily beaded, and a neckband of fur that denoted his rank as chief, which he wore during special functions such as this.

His thick, long hair hung down his back to his waist, and his headband, also of fur, matched his neckband. A lone eagle feather hung from a coil of his hair at the right side of his face.

"If you are restless, I can understand," Swift Horse said somewhat louder, yet in enough of a whisper that only she could hear. "The ceremony is long, but so shall ours be."

"I assure you that I won't be restless during our ceremony, for I so look forward to it," she whispered back to him. "I am so impressed by everything—by the people, the ceremony, and this lovely building. It is so huge."

"It took many days and nights to build it," Swift Horse said, looking with pride all around him, and then at the high, pointed ceiling. "One can feel the Master of Breath here."

His eyes were drawn quickly away from Marsha and again to his shaman as he was finalizing the ceremony.

"Our Supreme God, our Master of Breath, is the Father and Creator of us all, red as well as white," Bright Moon said, sliding his gaze past the two newlyweds and smiling at Abraham, who sat at Swift Horse's right side. "And he is also the Father and Creator of those whose skin is black."

Marsha looked around Swift Horse, at Abraham, and saw how he was beaming to have been singled out for a blessing during the ceremony.

"I appeal to the spirits of the universe—the sun, moon, and other of nature's spirits—to bless these two beloved people in marriage," Bright Moon said. His eyes fell upon Soft Wind, and then Edward James. He reached for their hands and placed one on the other, then placed his own on theirs. "I bless you," he said solemnly. "Go forth now and be happy."

Tears came to Marsha's eyes when she saw the joy and peace in her brother's eyes as he twined his arms around his wife's waist and drew her next to him, gave her a soft kiss, and then swept her up into his arms and swung her around, laughing merrily.

"My wife!" he cried. "Soft Wind, you are now my wife!"

Soft Wind clung to him, giggling, her long black hair flying around her face as Edward James took one more spin with her, the skirt of her long doeskin dress fluttering around her ankles.

Suddenly loud cheers, followed by chants, filled the huge chamber as the women left the rotunda and returned with all assortments of food. Soon everyone had their wooden plates filled— deer, peaches and apples, sweet potatoes, corn, and a variety of wild nuts and berries.

Marsha had left momentarily, then came back with a surprise for her brother and his new bride. She had baked a three-layered wedding cake that was covered with white icing. Of course it was not enough to feed everyone, but its presence drew gasps of wonder as the people gazed upon something they had never seen before.

"In my culture, it is custom to have a wedding cake," Marsha explained, then went and gave her brother and then Soft Wind a hug. "Congratulations. I hope you both will be happy."

"Thank you for the cake," Edward James said, holding his sister's hand as well as his bride's, as he looked over at Soft Wind and saw the look of awe in her eyes as she still gazed at the cake.

Marsha stood on tiptoe and whispered into her brother's ear. "Give her the first bite," she urged.

Edward James smiled and nodded, then took up a knife and sliced a piece from the cake. He turned to Soft Moon and gently placed the piece to her lips. She smiled up at him as she took a bite.

Marsha edged up close to Soft Wind and handed her a piece that she had sliced for her. "It is your turn to give your groom a bite," she said, glad when Soft Wind took the cake and did as she suggested.

Then Marsha addressed the crowd. "I wish there was enough for everyone," she said, smiling around the room at the Creek people. "But I'm sure you see that there is only enough for the bride and groom."

Everyone nodded, then Swift Horse stepped up to Marsha's side. "Those who wish to dance can go where a huge fire has been built at the outskirts of the village where there are less trees!" he shouted. "It is a time of merriment!"

People began filing out of the building until everyone was gone except for Edward James, Soft Wind, Marsha, and Swift Horse.

"I am ready to dance!" Soft Wind announced as she grabbed Edward James by an arm. "Come. Let us dance with the others!"

Edward James gave her a wary look. "But are you strong enough?" he asked, smoothing a lock of fallen hair back from her flushed cheeks.

"I am strong enough to do anything, especially now that I have my husband to do it with," Soft Wind said, her eyes brilliantly wide, her smile radiant. "I am so happy, Edward James. Oh, so happy!"

Edward James drew her into his arms and kissed her, then gave Swift Horse a wink as he gazed across Soft Wind's shoulder at him, then took Soft Wind's hand and left the rotunda.

Marsha turned to Swift Horse. She gazed up at him, smiling. "And what was that wink for?" she asked softly.

"It is because I told him that we would not join the dancing, but instead go elsewhere to be alone," Swift Horse said, taking her hands, drawing her closer. "Or do you wish to dance, instead?"

"I doubt that I know how to dance your people's dances, and even if I did, you know that I would rather be with you," Marsha murmured. She thrilled when he brought his lips down onto hers and gave her a passionate kiss, causing a tremoring warmth to enter her belly.

"I have made a special place for us," he then whispered against her lips. "Tonight some might think we are the newlyweds, not my sister and your brother."

A quick blush heated Marsha's cheeks as she looked into his eyes, then walked hand-in-hand with him from the rotunda, her insides warmed through and through by what Swift Horse seemed to be implying—that they would be making love!

She had been taught that it was not right to make love before vows were spoken, but strangely enough, she did feel as though she were already this wonderful man's wife. And soon they would be married, so nothing would dissuade her from what she expected to happen only moments from now.

As they stepped outside, Marsha could hear

music and laughter. She gazed up at Swift Horse. "It does sound like fun," she murmured.

"We can still go there, if you wish," Swift Horse said, trying not to show his disappointment.

But he understood that this must be her first time to make love, and perhaps she was bashful and hesitant to do so.

"I would like to take a quick look, if you don't mind," Marsha said, truly needing more time now that she knew what lay ahead. What if she wasn't a skilled enough lover? If she disappointed him, would he even want her as his wife?

She felt some apprehension, but she knew that she wanted to go through with it, for she had had a strange sort of hunger inside her after having met Swift Horse, and she had to believe those hungers were sexual.

He took her by the hand and walked her into the village.

They stood back and watched, Marsha all eyes. She smiled when she found Edward James with Soft Wind among the dancers, amazed at how skilled her brother was with this sort of dancing, which was so vastly different from that which he had been taught in Georgia.

With the accompaniment of skin-covered

wooden and pottery drums, gourd and turtle-shell rattles, and a singer, men and women, separately or together, danced in a slow shuffle or wildly animated motions. Suddenly scores of shell-shaker girls joined the men in a dance with a rapid tempo, the sound now almost deafening.

"Dances of my people are called *obangas* in our Creek language," Swift Horse said, twining an arm around her waist. "Do you wish to learn today, or another day?"

Marsha gazed up at him and saw how he looked so wistfully into her eyes and knew why. "Later," she murmured, placing a gentle hand on his cheek. "We have a lifetime of *obangas* to join."

Smiling broadly, he took her hand, swung her away from the crowd, and led her to the horses he had already prepared for riding.

"Where are we going?" Marsha asked as he helped her into her saddle.

His only response was to smile at her.

Chapter 28

Love and harmony combine,
And around our souls entwine. . . .
———William Blake

With dusk falling all around them, Marsha and Swift Horse rode up a slight incline, and then across a straight stretch of land again.

She was familiar now with where they were traveling, having been there one other time with Swift Horse.

She gazed over at him, smiling, when she now heard the splash of water and knew that the waterfall was close. She would never forget her other time there with him. It had been so wonderful to sit with him, talking and kissing.

Soon she would even be his bride. She knew the hardships that came with a white woman loving a man with copper skin——that she would be cast from the white world as someone contagious, for it was taboo for a white woman to marry an Indian.

"You are so quiet," Swift Horse said, turning his eyes to Marsha and catching her gazing at him.

"Yes, I'm quiet, but my mind is spinning with thoughts of so many things," she said, smiling at him.

"Your brother and my sister?" Swift Horse asked, smiling, too.

"Yes, and you and me," Marsha said. She would not admit to all of those negative things that she was thinking. She only wanted to think and feel positive about everything.

"I, too, have been thinking about you," Swift Horse said, sidling his horse over closer to hers. "Since we met, it has been hard for me to think about much else."

"But you are a powerful chief whose mind must not stray too long from your duties," Marsha said, the roar of the falls so much closer now.

"In the life of a chief, his people do come ahead of anyone else, until a woman enters this chief's heart and life," Swift Horse explained. "And then the woman comes first. A chief's people would not deny their leader the part of his heart that is given away to a woman that he loves and plans to marry. It is known that a man leads better if he has a woman who feeds his needs other than those placed in his life by his people. A woman ofttimes makes a leader even stronger, for the man feeds from this love of a woman, which in turn makes him stronger in mind and body."

"I hope your people accept me as that woman," Marsha murmured. "When I become your wife I do not want to ever get in the way of your duties to your people."

"You will never be seen as someone being in the way," Swift Horse said, then saw how she again gazed ahead, spotting where a campfire and blankets awaited their arrival.

He had come before the ceremony and prepared things for their time together, having made a fire large enough to ensure it would still be burning upon their arrival. He saw that it had now burned down to how he wished it to be while they sat by the falls discussing things and then . . .

And then made love, he thought.

They rode onward and drew a tight rein beside the falls, the campfire warm against Marsha's flesh as she dismounted near it.

She held on to her reins and watched Swift Horse take his horse to a tree a short distance from the camp and secure his reins to a low limb, then come and take her horse and do the same.

Dusk was sending sprays of various colors of pink across the horizon in the distance. A coyote barked on the other side of the falls, waiting for dark.

Marsha shivered at the sound. "Are we safe here after it is dark?" she asked Swift Horse as he knelt and placed more wood in the fire.

"While you are with me, you will always be safe," Swift Horse said. He rose and took her by a hand and led her down beside the fire.

"That coyote. Is it calling to others that might be on this side of the falls?" Marsha asked, snuggling closer to him as they sat side-by-side on the thick pallet of blankets.

"Did you hear a response?" Swift Horse said, lifting a folded blanket and placing it around both their shoulders, so that their shoulders touched beneath it.

"No," Marsha said, glad that she wasn't hearing the one animal any longer, either.

"Relax and enjoy our moments together," Swift Horse said, reaching beneath the blanket and taking one of her hands. "Are you warm enough?"

"Yes, and I am so content to be here with you," Marsha murmured. She looked on both sides of her and then at the falls as the water splashed downward into the river below. "You brought me to a different place beside the falls the last time," she murmured, questioning him with her eyes.

"It is even more beautiful here, do you not think so?" Swift Horse said, gesturing around him with a hand. "Do you see the flower that grows in such abundance along the slope of land that leads downward to the river below?"

"Yes," Marsha murmured, having noticed it the moment they arrived.

It was a beautiful creamy-white trumpet-shaped flower that sent off a lemony scent and seemed to glow now in the twilight hour of evening. The flowers seemed even to be flaunting their scent, their curvy shape, their luminous color.

She looked quickly over at Swift Horse. "I have never seen such a gorgeous flower as this."

"I know this plant well," Swift Horse said, somewhat frowning. "Its name is Sacred Datura. Normally it is a desert plant, but long ago an Indian tribe called the Zuni brought it here and planted it in the ground for their personal use. It has spread like wildfire in this area, but my people know to avoid it, and so must you. Do not even touch it, and especially don't smell of its flower."

"Why?" Marsha asked, her eyes widening. "You talk of it as though it is a devil's plant."

"That is a good reference to describe it," Swift Horse said. "The Zuni used this flower as a hallucinogen by soaking and steeping the leaves into a tea, or chewing the seeds or roots to get the same effect."

"Good Lord," Marsha gasped. "I am so glad you told me, or I might have put some in a vase on my brother's kitchen table."

"There is a myth about the flower that is told to children," Swift Horse said. "Do you wish to hear the myth?"

"Yes, very much," Marsha said, sliding the blanket from around her shoulders and sitting directly in front of Swift Horse, her eyes wide as she awaited hearing the story. She loved these special moments with him, when she had the chance to learn about him and his people.

"The myth states that when the earth was still soft, two curious Zuni children spied on the gods and later gossiped about the secrets they saw," he began, the blanket no longer around his shoulders, either, but instead resting around his waist. "The twin war gods were so upset that they caused the earth to swallow up the children.

At the place where they disappeared, the Sacred Datura grew and blossomed for the first time. In my teachings, I tell the children that the use of this plant, even by experienced shamans such as Bright Moon, is considered dangerous. Visions can turn into convulsions—or death."

"How horrible," Marsha said, moving back to sit beside Swift Horse, again staring at the flowers.

"This sinister flower has become part of my understanding of the natural world, where beauty and violence often intertwine," Swift Horse said hoarsely. "I must say, though, that the beautiful white trumpets of this Sacred Datura evoke in me a physical response—a slight hollowness in the chest, a momentary stillness."

Marsha started to tell him just how beautiful what he said was, but stopped and gasped when she saw something else that seemed surreal. Out of the twilight came a fast-flying, white-lined sphinx moth, stopping and hovering over a flower, feeding from it.

It hovered while feeding, its wings a white whir as it sipped nectar from the deep white tube, then whirled away like a spinning dervish. It became a blur in the air for a moment, and then poised itself before another flower, sipping nectar again, its heavy body keeping aloft by the beating of its narrow wings.

Swift Horse also watched the moth. "Each flower on a Sacred Datura plant blooms for only one night," he said. "During those brief hours, the large, silky, trumpet-shaped blossom must do everything it can to attract a suitor, one who will sip the sugary nectar at the base of the florel tube, pick up grains of pollen, and carry these off to fertilize another flower on another Sacred Datura. For this reason, alone, the petals open at twilight."

And then the moth was gone again, along with it the mystery.

"I have just witnessed something so beautiful, it is hard to describe it. I'm so glad you told me," Marsha murmured, then melted inside when he drew her even closer and lowered his lips to her mouth.

All thoughts and wonder of plants and flowers and lovely moths were wiped away. All Marsha was aware of was how her pulse raced and how her insides were mushy warm from Swift Horse's kiss and embrace. She was only slightly aware of being undressed, and of lying on the blankets. Swift Horse was soon nude, too, and blanketed her with his body.

It was all natural, how they came together, as

though they had done this thousands of times before—how she knew the art of pleasing him even though this was her very first time with a man in this way. Even the pain that came with her losing her virginity to this man was instant.

Now past that pain and the newness of making love for the first time in her life, pleasure spread through her body as he kissed and stroked her where she had not known she had feelings before. Her every secret place became his.

His meltingly hot kiss as he plunged into her, withdrew and plunged again, made her writhe in response, becoming someone new to her herself—someone whose soft moans were repeatedly surfacing from deep inside her.

Her senses were reeling as she clung to his rock hardness, then sucked in a wild breath of an even more intense pleasure when he slid his lips downward from her mouth and he rolled first one of her nipples with his tongue, and then the other.

His tongue, his mouth, his hands, his manhood, worked their magic on her, causing waves of liquid heat to pulse through her. She was experiencing desire such as she had never known before as sweet currents of warmth swept through her, over and over again, as his lean, sinewy buttocks moved rhythmically.

Swift Horse's body was growing feverish. He had not expected such intense passion as this woman evoked within him. He moved his lips from hers and lay his cheek against hers, trying to draw air into his lungs. He was almost beyond coherent thought as he found himself climbing to that place where paradise awaited them both. He had felt the pressure building from somewhere deep inside him, growing hotter like a fire consuming him.

Swift Horse leaned away from her so that their eyes could meet. "Do you know now how much I want you?" he said huskily as he gazed into her passion-clouded eyes. "Can you feel it? Can you even taste it?"

"Yes, I feel all of those things," Marsha murmured, her heart pounding in her own ears. "I never knew making love could be this overwhelmingly beautiful."

"And you have not even experienced the ultimate of pleasure yet," Swift Horse said, smiling into her eyes. "My woman . . . are you ready?"

Marsha knew that her face must be flushed, for she seemed consumed by heat from her head to her toes. She was filled with a longing never known by her before, and as his lips came down hard onto hers and he plunged into her again and began thrusting, heated contractions of pleasure knifed through her, over and over again, filling her with a pleasure too magnificent to describe.

She opened herself wider to him. Her hips responded to his thrusts, in her own rhythmic movement, and her whole body began to quiver. Her mind seemed to splinter into many explosions of color as sensations such as she never knew could exist swam through her. She clung to him as his body thrust more deeply inside her, over and over again, as he moaned and held her endearingly close, his lips now buried against the curve of her neck.

And then when it was over, they both lay clinging to each other, their breaths mingling as they gazed into each other's eyes.

"How could such wondrous feelings exist?" Marsha said breathlessly, still seeming to be pulsing where she had just been awakened to the full pleasure of making love.

"What we shared together was borne of our love for each other," Swift Horse said, reaching a hand to her brow and wiping a pearl of sweat from her flesh. "It is something we shall always have. When night falls, the bed will beckon for us. When the sun rises in early morn, we will not want even then to leave the bed."

"But your chieftain duties will always be awaiting you," Marsha said, smiling into his eyes.

"Not before we make love," Swift Horse said, laughing huskily.

"It will be wonderful to go to sleep at night after making love and start my day making love," Marsha said, finding it hard to envision such happiness. But she had discovered that such things were possible now that she had found paradise in the arms of this lover who would soon be her husband.

"And then sometimes I will come to you midday to make love," Swift Horse said, laughing to himself when he saw how that remark made her eyes widen in wonder.

"That will be rare," he said, chuckling. "But if you ever wish for those moments, any time of the day, just reach your hand out for me and I will be there for you."

A movement behind them in the brush caused Marsha to tense up and to grab a blanket and cover herself. She sat up and peered into the darkness that had now come down around them in what seemed to be a black cloak, for there was no moon tonight, nor stars.

"It was only a night creature seeking companionship, too," Swift Horse said, reassuring her that no one was there spying on them, yet he, too, gazed into the darkness to reassure himself.

"Whatever it was is gone," Swift Horse said, then placed his hands at her waist and drew her onto his lap.

He wrapped his arms around her and kissed her, and soon everything but their lovemaking was forgotten.

Chapter 29

Marsha sat on a platform with Swift Horse, witnessing the Green Corn Ceremony. She learned that the Creek life was filled with ceremony and celebration. The return of hunters meant that a villagewide dance and feast of bear ribs barbecued with honey would be held.

But she now knew that the most important of all Creek ceremonial occasions was the *Boskita*, Busk, or Green Corn Ceremony, celebrated annually when the new maize had ripened and was ready for harvesting, as well as marking the beginning of a new year of plenty.

During the festival, a new fire was lit, the green corn was roasted, and a new year commenced.

The sacred fire of four logs represented the sun, the giver of life to the maize. The corn goddess, maize, fire, and the sun were all vital parts of Creek religion.

Tonight, as Marsha sat with Swift Horse, the moon high overhead, dancers performed around the huge outdoor fire, where earlier in the afternoon a part of the new harvest had been sacrificed, to the accompaniment of drums, rattles, and a flute made from the tibia of a deer's leg.

Marsha was astounded tonight by the dress of the women. They wore the usual dress, but what was new to Marsha was how they had dressed their legs in a kind of leather stockings, hung full of the hoofs of the roe deer in the form of bells. In addition, the women wore earrings, bracelets, and other ornaments, all of which made a variety of sounds that wafted into the night air.

Although Marsha was intrigued by everything that had happened today, she could not focus totally on it. She glanced over at Swift Horse, whose eyes were slowly scanning the crowd.

She knew whom he was missing.

One Eye.

As the sun had set in the west, all of the separate Creek clans had finally arrived. They sat in a wide, half circle around the fire, enjoying the dancing and music, and would soon enjoy a feast of feasts with Swift Horse's clan.

As people had begun arriving, Swift Horse had greeted them personally, his eyes watching for One Eye's arrival with his clan. One Eye's clan had been the last to arrive—in fact they were so late that Swift Horse was not standing there to greet them. He had already sat down on the platform with Marsha and would remain there until the dancing part of the celebration was over.

Marsha knew that Swift Horse realized something was awry when the Wolf Clan arrived so late.

Knowing how Swift Horse felt about not seeing One Eye there, Marsha could almost feel his anger. His longtime best friend had not attended the ceremony—the first time he had not attended with his clan, ever.

Marsha jumped with a start when Swift Horse suddenly left the platform. She looked over at Soft Wind, who sat at her left side, and questioned her with her eyes as Soft Wind looked back at her.

"Go to him," Soft Wind softly urged, nodding. "He needs you."

Trusting that Soft Wind knew the protocol of things and was urging Marsha to leave, Marsha

nodded, smiled at Soft Wind, then left the platform in a rush, hurriedly following in the direction that she had seen Swift Horse go in
determined, angry steps.

When she finally reached him at the corral, his
hands were tightly fisted at his sides, and his
eyes stared straight ahead.

Marsha stepped gingerly to his side. "Swift
Horse?" she said, reaching and touching his arm.
When he didn't respond, she stepped between
him and where he was gazing, so that he would
see her.

"You finally know, don't you?" Marsha murmured, reaching a gentle hand to his cheek. "Because of One Eye's absence at the most
important ceremony of the year, you know that
he is sporting an injury that I inflicted on him."

"I believe that now, too, from the depths of my
heart, but still I cannot face him with it," Swift
Horse said. He took her hand in his. "My
woman, I must still wait and let him reveal himself to *me*. He will not be able to bear silence between us for much longer, not after having been
confidantes and best friends for so long."

"But while you are waiting for him to come to
you, might he not be wreaking havoc somewhere else as he is prone to do?" Marsha asked,
searching his eyes. "Can you chance that?"

"I am certain that the wound you inflicted on him has slowed him down enough for me not to have that burden on my mind," Swift Horse explained. "I must wait, Marsha. He will not be able to bear absence from my village for long, for it has become his second home. And when he is able to travel, I feel this will be the first place he will come."

"But the wound," Marsha said, not wanting to argue, yet feeling the need to. "He knows his wound will reveal his guilt. The scar will always be proof, for I hit him hard enough for him to have a scar left there forever."

"He is a clever man who will come up with an answer to even that," Swift Horse said, slowly shaking his head back and forth. "He is more clever than I ever gave him credit for."

"Yet you will not act on knowing that?" Marsha asked, but when she saw the added torment those words caused in his eyes, she flung herself into his arms. "I'm sorry. I won't say anything else about this. You know what you are doing."

His arms swept around her. He leaned his face into hers. "My woman, do not ever be sorry about anything you say to me, for everything you say is from the heart," he said passionately. "And I understand how you must want this thing finished once and for all. But I do need this time."

"And I promise you that you will not hear another word from me about it," Marsha murmured.

Realizing the music was over and the dancing had stopped, and that everyone should now be entering the council house to eat the feast that had been set out by all of the women of the village, Swift Horse took Marsha by the hand. "We must join the others again," he said, already walking away from the corral with her.

"Everyone will wonder where we went, and why," Marsha said, remembering how everyone had watched him leave, and then feeling those same eyes on her as she left.

"But no one will ask," Swift Horse said tightly. "They know that their chief would leave the celebration only if he felt a strong need to. No one questions what I do, or why."

"Except me," Marsha said, giving him an apologetic look as his eyes met with hers.

"You are my woman and should have the freedom to question me about anything," he said, then forced a smile when he came to a small crowd of his people who had not yet entered the huge council house to join the others to eat. "The corn awaits us," Swift Horse said, gesturing toward the opened council house door, where the scent of an assortment of food wafted from within. They all went inside.

Soon Marsha and Swift Horse were sitting amidst everyone else, their wooden trays piled with an assortment of food, corn the most prominent.

Marsha now knew also about *Sofkee,* a gruel or soup, to which pieces of venison were added. She knew now that hardly a Creek household was without a *Sofkee* pot.

She knew that sunflower seeds and honey from bee trees were a favorite among the Creek community and that sweet potatoes were almost as important as corn, delicious when nuts were added to the sweet potato dishes.

"My brother, I saw you leave," Soft Wind said as she came and sat beside Swift Horse. "Is everything all right now?"

"My sister, nothing will be absolutely all right again until I have solved the problem of One Eye," Swift Horse said, only loud enough for her to hear. "But do not worry yourself about it. In time I will have all of the answers I seek."

Marsha stiffened when two warriors from One Eye's village came and stood before Swift Horse, causing him to rise and gaze slowly from one to the other.

"Our chief sent word to you of his regrets for having not been able to attend the ceremony today," Night Moon said. "He is not a well man. But he says he will be well soon and will come for council with you."

"You say he is not a well man," Swift Horse said guardedly. "What ails him?"

"He spoke from inside his cabin to us, so we did not see him," Night Moon answered. "And he did not say. Why do you question such a thing?"

"I do not like to think that my friend is ill, and I hope it is not something serious," Swift Horse said, lying. "Go back to him and give him my regards and tell him that I will want to meet him in private council, as we ofttimes do, when he is well enough to come to me."

"Might you want to go to him?" Night Moon asked.

"If he is not well enough to attend today's ceremony, he will not be well enough for friends to come and take him from his sickbed," Swift Horse quickly responded. He placed a gentle hand on Night Moon's shoulder. "Just go and tell him what I have said."

Night Moon nodded, then rejoined his clan's group and continued with the feast.

"And so he is too ill to attend the ceremony, is he?" Marsha said sarcastically.

Swift Horse said nothing, then smiled when a young brave came with a huge platter of food. "I am taking this to Abraham, if that is all right," the brave said, his eyes dancing. "I talked to him earlier. He said he is too tired for such a vigorous celebration."

"Yes, I know, but I am certain he will feel better soon," Swift Horse said, having gone to check on Abraham earlier. He hated seeing just how long it was taking for the man to get stronger. But in time he would be as good as new.

"Then I can take him food?" the brave asked, his eyes wide. "I like to sit and talk with him and pet the fawn."

Swift Horse patted the child's head. "Yes, go and take the food," he said. "You are a thoughtful brave, you are."

Marsha smiled as the child ran from the huge house, then looked quickly over at Swift Horse as he took her plate from her hands, set it aside, and led her from the council house.

"Come with me," he said. "My people no longer need me. They are enjoying the food and company of the other clans."

Marsha smiled down at Edward James and

Soft Wind, gave them a soft wave of good-bye, then went outside with Swift Horse.

He turned to her and gazed at her, the huge outdoor fire's glow shining in his eyes. "I need you," he said thickly.

She didn't have to be told any more than that. She went with him to his cabin, and moved into his arms when the door was locked to everyone else.

"I have waited for this moment all day long," he said huskily, then gave her a kiss that melted her insides.

When he lifted her into his arms, she placed her cheek on his chest as he took her to his bedroom and lay her gently on his bed of blankets.

She watched him undress as the fire cast dancing shadows all around him on the walls, on the ceilings, and then on his nakedness.

Chapter 30

Let knowledge grow from more to more,
But more of reverence in us dwell.
—Alfred, Lord Tennyson

The merriment and feasting momentarily forgotten, Swift Horse and Marsha lay together on
his bed.

"When we are together, it is only us . . . no one
else, nothing else," Swift Horse said huskily as
he gave Marsha an endearing look, the shine of
the fire in her violet eyes. "You take me away
from all wrongs. You make everything right
again."

"Without you, nothing would be right," Marsha murmured. "My darling Swift Horse, make
love with me. Bring the stars and the heavens all
around us as a gentle embrace—as our *haven*."
Pleasure spread through Marsha when Swift
Horse filled her with his heat and began slowly
thrusting into her, his lips now on hers.

A raging hunger overcame Marsha as she clung to Swift Horse and tasted his lips. His hands eagerly and hungrily searched her body, and then cupped a breast and kneaded it until Marsha's pleasure became intermingled with a sweet sort of pain.

The hot touch of his body against hers and the way his lean, sinewy buttocks moved in such a steady rhythm made a passion burn higher within her. She grew feverish as he cradled her now, their bodies molded together and moving rhythmically as one.

Swift Horse groaned as he felt the tightness in his loins coil intensely as he moved within Marsha slowly, yet deliberately. His tongue brushed her lips lightly, his eyes dark and stormy as he gazed down at her.

"Kiss me again . . . hold me more tightly," Marsha whispered, her ankles locked about him as his lips bore down upon her in a savage kiss.

When he moved, she moved. When the pleasure began to peak for one, it did for the other. They clung and rocked together as that ultimate joy was reached and savored, then they lay still together, breathing hard.

"I am so glad for my brother," she murmured. "And also for your sister. Wasn't their ceremony such a glorious sight to see? Their happiness is the same as ours, Swift Horse. And soon we will say vows that will make our own happiness complete."

His hand made a slow, sensuous descent along her spine as he gazed at her, his face now a mask of naked desire. "I had not known such a love as ours could exist—such a woman as you could exist," he said. His gaze moved slowly over her, as though in a caress, seeing her perfect in every way.

He bent his lips to a breast and drew a nipple between his lips and flicked his tongue around it, drawing a sensual moan from within her. He moved over her again, their bodies straining together. His hands wove through her silken hair as he drew her lips to his.

Marsha's pulse raced as she felt his manhood filling her again. "Every breath I take is yours," she whispered against his lips. "Please, oh, please never stop loving me."

A soft cry of passion escaped from between her parted lips as he plunged his hardness inside her. As his dark, stormy eyes gazed at her, she placed a hand to his cheek and smiled at him as he began his easy strokes within her. Her breathing grew ragged when his hands cupped her breasts and his thumbs circled her nipples, drawing them into tautness.

Marsha twined her arms around his neck and urged his lips to hers. Passion erupted between them as they kissed, their tongues meeting as their lips parted.

With an instinct for pleasure now that had been borne within her that first moment of Swift Horse's showing her the true meaning of love, her hips moved in unison with his eager thrusts. Raking her fingernails down his back, she moved her hands to his buttocks and splayed her fingers across his hard body. She urged him closer, reveling in the feel of his wondrous thrusts inside her.

And then he slowed his body and withdrew his hardness, breathing heavily as he pressed his lips to the delicate column of her throat.

"I never want our time together like this to end," he said huskily. "But the real world always awaits us."

"Not yet," she said, kissing him.

They moved together again for a moment longer, then again went over the edge that overwhelmed them both, the pleasure so intense, so wondrous to behold. And then they lay quietly together again, only now aware of the laughter outside the lodge, and remembering the celebration of renewal—the beginning of a new Creek year.

"My people celebrate the new year at another time than you do, and in a different way," Marsha murmured, aching when she recalled those New Year's Eves with her parents, and how her mother always made black-eyed peas the next day, a ritual she never forgot. They gave hope to the new year, her mother had always told her.

"Will you spend the night with me?" Swift Horse suddenly blurted out. "Your brother and his new bride might need their privacy."

"Yes, I had thought of that, too, since our cabin is not all that large," Marsha said, remembering how her brother had cleaned up his own bedroom on the day of his wedding, shocking Marsha to no end when she watched from the door as he struggled to put the sheets on the bed.

"Then you will stay?" Swift Horse asked, gently touching her cheek.

"Yes, I will stay," Marsha murmured, cuddling closer to him.

She hated it when she yawned, but it had been a long and tiring day and she only now realized how exhausted she was.

"You are tired," Swift Horse said softly. "Sleep, my woman. I shall hold you as you sleep."

"Then I shall dream of angels all night long," she said, laughing softly.

"Angels?" he asked, searching her eyes.

"Mother always told me to dream of angels when she tucked me in at night when I was a child," she murmured. "That was the same as telling me to sleep in peace and love."

"And did you?" he asked, smoothing a fallen lock of hair back from her face.

"Always, until—" she said, her voice breaking.

"Until when?" he said, yet thinking he knew the answer. When her parents had died, that part of her that gave her peace at night had surely died, as well.

"Until my parents died," she blurted out. Tears filling her eyes, she turned and clung to him. "But now I have you," she said, her voice breaking. "Hold me, darling. Hold me and never let me go."

He pulled her closer to him and held her there until he saw that she was asleep, then sighed deeply and gave in to sleep himself.

While he slept, he dreamed. In that dream he was in a cave, lit on all sides by torches burning brightly. These torches were lined up all along the walls on both sides, seemingly there to lead him to something.

He was alone. He felt the dampness of the

cave all around him, and saw an occasional bat fly around his head, then disappear.

And then he saw something else. He saw a trunk at the far back of the cave. He hurried to it.

When he reached it, he bent to his knees and slowly opened the lid, then gasped and almost fell backward when he discovered scalps, jewelry—the sort that white people wore, intermingled—and so many other things that only an evil person would place there—someone who enjoyed killing and taking scalps.

There were many more things there, but Swift Horse was aware of something else—the crash of water from somewhere behind him.

Then he recognized it to be the sound of a waterfall.

He knew now that he was behind the waterfall that he loved, and that whoever had brought this trunk into this cave had done so by having stepped behind the waterfall to find a cave that Swift Horse had never been aware of.

He awakened in a sweat, so abruptly that it had disturbed Marsha. She leaned up on an elbow and gazed at him.

She saw that he was covered with sweat and she saw a look of horror in his eyes.

"Did you have a bad dream?" she asked, reaching a gentle hand to his face, then drew her hand away. "Darling, you are covered with sweat. Tell me. What did you dream about?"

"There is a cave behind the waterfall," he blurted out, suddenly sitting up. He stroked his hands through his thick hair, bringing it back over his shoulders.

He turned to her. "The waterfall where we have made love?" he said. "In my dream, I discovered that someone else has been there."

"I'm sure there has been," Marsha said, sitting up beside him. "It's such a lovely place."

"Perhaps not," Swift Horse said thickly. "You see, we sat there and enjoyed the falls. If my dream, which is always the same as my visions, is true, someone used the falls in a very different, evil way."

"But how?" Marsha asked, drawing a blanket up and around her shoulders.

"Often my dreams—my visions—are true," Swift Horse said. "If so, what I dreamed tonight is also true. If I go to the waterfall tomorrow, I will surely find a cave behind it. And in that cave I will surely find a trunk."

"A trunk?" Marsha asked, searching his eyes, which seemed haunted.

"It is filled with many things that only an evil man would place there," Swift Horse said, his voice breaking. "I saw scalps, jewelry that had to have been taken from white people . . ."

A shiver of disgust rippled across Marsha's flesh. She hugged herself with her arms. "Do you think those things were placed there by the one-eyed man—by One Eye?" she asked guardedly.

"I will soon know," he said determinedly.

"What are you going to do?" she asked, watching as he drew a blanket around his own shoulders.

"I will not disturb my people's celebration tonight, but tomorrow is another day and the celebration will be behind us," he said. "Tomorrow I will go and see if my dreams are real again. I will see if there is a cave behind the falls."

"Won't it be dangerous to go behind the falls?" Marsha asked softly.

"There is danger in many things, but when answers are needed, the fear of danger is not a problem," he said, staring into the flames of the fire. "But if I do find what my dreams showed to me, yes, I believe it will be the work of the one-eyed man."

He turned to her with determination in his eyes. "It will be the work of One Eye," he said, finding it hard, himself, that he now truly believed that the man who was his friend for so long was the one who committed the crimes he was now being accused of.

"Finally you believe me," Marsha said, dropping the blanket from around her. She flung herself into his arms, causing his own blanket to flutter down around his waist.

"May I go with you tomorrow?" Marsha blurted out.

"Yes, you can accompany me there," he replied. "It is only right that you do. You see, I owe you an apology for not having listened to you from the beginning. I will repay you in every way that I can. Tomorrow is the beginning of those ways."

"Thank you," she said, tears filling her eyes.

Then she crept into his arms again and found peace and love within them, her cheek pressed against his powerful chest so comforting to her.

Chapter 31

O, let me once more rest
My soul upon that dazzling breast.
                    —John Keats

The day was gray, with low-hanging clouds and a smell of rain in the air, as Marsha rode with Swift Horse and several of his warriors toward the waterfall. She hated that perhaps her happy memories of this place were going to be clouded by something sinister, for if Swift Horse's dream, or vision, was true, nothing about the waterfall would ever be beautiful again.

She was dressed today in her leather riding skirt, a leather jacket, and butter-soft boots and gloves, to ward off the chill of the morning. Her hair was drawn back from her face with a yellow bow, to keep her hair from blowing in her eyes on this windy day.

As they rode onward, they could hear the

splash of the waterfall through the trees up ahead. A chill rippled along Marsha's flesh.

They had arrived at the waterfall.

On this day, when everything was ugly and gray, the waterfall still held its beauty. As it splashed downward, many rainbows were created, the colors so beautiful it almost made Marsha forget the ugliness that could come into one's life at the hands of a madman!

"I will investigate first," Swift Horse said, quickly dismounting his steed.

He tied the reins to a low limb, gazed solemnly at Marsha as he came to help her from her horse, then held her in his arms and gazed into her eyes.

"Soon this will all be over," he said. "If I find the proof of One Eye's crime, we shall take the trunk to Fort Hill."

"And then who will be responsible for making the one-eyed man—for making One Eye—pay for his crimes?" Marsha said, almost chokingly as she returned Swift Horse's steady gaze. "He must pay dearly, you know."

"Yes, I know, and he will," Swift Horse said tightly.

"*One Eye* will pay," she softly corrected. "Not just 'he' or not just the 'one-eyed man.' Swift

Horse, One Eye *is* the one who is guilty of these terrible things. Soon you will see."

"I already know it is he," Swift Horse said, his voice drawn. "I just need this proof before confronting him."

"Darling, there is already enough proof and you know it," Marsha said, searching his eyes now. She could see how hard he was struggling with this, and she understood, yet it was time for his struggles to end and for him to openly say what the reality was. But she would not force the issue.

Swift Horse brushed a soft kiss across her brow, then turned and trotted to the falls. He began to inch along a small outcropping of rock to investigate behind the falls.

When his moccasined foot slipped on the wet rock, Marsha gasped and covered her mouth with a hand. Her heart resumed its normal beats when she saw that he had grabbed on to a large, thick tree root that was growing from out of the wall of rock. He steadied himself, then took only two more steps and stopped.

His heart stopped for a moment when he did see an opening ahead, an opening that surely did lead into a cave.

"It is here!" he shouted. "There is a cave!"

Marsha's pulse raced as the other warriors ran

toward the ledge from which Swift Horse had stepped and was now coming back. When he reached Marsha, he placed his hands on her shoulders.

"It is too dangerous for you to go there. There is not much room for one to walk, and the rocky ledge is wet. I would rather you stay—"

She slipped a quick hand over his mouth. "No, I can't stay here by myself and you know why," she blurted out. "Who is to say that One Eye is not watching even now? If I am left alone . . ."

He reached for her hand and removed it from his face and nodded. "I was foolish even to think about leaving you alone," he said, turning and seeing that the warriors, who were surely already inside the cave, were no longer in sight, leaving no one to stay with Marsha. He gazed into her eyes again. "I will keep you safe," he said softly. "Come. You walk ahead of me along the ledge. I will keep hold of you."

Marsha swallowed hard and nodded, then went with him to the ledge. Only now did she truly see and feel the danger of what she was doing with Swift Horse. The soles of her boots were smooth and each step she took on the wet ledge was a true challenge. But she continued onward, the feel of Swift Horse's arm around her waist giving her the courage to make that final step into the cave.

She was filled with wonder when she saw many torches lighted along the walls of the cave, splashing their wavering, golden light along the ceiling, floor, and walls. She gave Swift Horse a questioning look.

"He must have been here recently, or how else would the torches have been lit?" he said, eyeing the long row of burning torches. "I doubt they would last for long, not with the wind and the dampness blowing into the cave."

"Yes, it is terribly damp . . . and cold," Marsha said, hugging herself in an effort to ward off as much of the chill as she could.

"Your vision was true! The trunk is here!" Sharp Nose's voice from the far end of the cave came to them as though in an echo.

"It contains many things bad!" Sharp Nose then shouted.

"Oh, no," Marsha said, a cold shudder of dread racing through her. She thought of the possibilities of something of her parents' being in that damnable trunk. Yet she did not see how those renegades who came out of the shadows of the trees on the one side of the road that day could have had time to take any "mementoes," for they had come and slaughtered, then had gone on their way.

"Do you want to stay here as I go get the trunk?" Swift Horse asked, placing gentle hands at her waist.

"No, I would be too afraid to stay alone, even this close to you," she said, her voice breaking. She looked over her shoulder at the cave's entrance, and at the water splashing in front of it, the rainbows no longer there, but instead, the image of One Eye laughingly staring back at her. She closed her eyes as she turned back to Swift Horse, then slowly opened them again.

"I would rather go with you," she blurted out.

He took her by a hand, and as they walked past the burning torches, Marsha forced from her mind what she might see.

As they approached the trunk, the warriors were standing around it, gazing down inside it. Sharp Nose knelt at its side, his eyes now on Marsha as a warning of sorts that she must not look.

She recalled one part of the dream that Swift Horse had described to her.

A scalp.

A scalp had been in the trunk!

What if . . . ?

No!

It couldn't be her parents! When they were rescued from where they had lain after the murder, they had, thankfully, their scalps. They were buried with their scalps. But seeing anyone's scalp would be traumatic. It would be so gruesome!

Now standing over the trunk, the glow of the torches reaching inside it, Marsha had to force herself to look. And when she did, everything within Marsha found the peace of knowing that she saw nothing of her parents there.

Then Swift Horse examined the contents of the trunk, rose to his feet, and looked from warrior to warrior. "I see nothing here that points to anyone in particular's guilt," he said with a relief in his voice that Marsha dreaded hearing. If he didn't absolutely see the proof he had wanted to see, then did he doubt all over again One Eye's role in the murders?

"But . . ." Swift Horse said, his jaw tightening. "There is a way to know who placed it here. The lit torches prove that someone comes often. I imagine the guilty one comes to gloat over what he has taken from those he had killed."

He looked over his shoulder, toward the cave's entrance, then around him again, at his warriors. "I imagine he was here even moments before our arrival," Swift Horse said. "He might have heard the horses and fled just in time. He might even now be out there, watching."

"Should we go and search for him?" Sharp Nose asked.

"No. Let him come to us. Let us catch him in the act. We will post a nearby sentry." He sighed heavily. "But the one I appoint must keep a close watch, for the guilty one will surely attempt to kill him," he said. "And then he would destroy the trunk so that it could not be taken to the white authorities."

"But it might take several days for One Eye to show himself," Marsha said, still wishing that Swift Horse would just go to One Eye's village and stop this nonsense right now!

"Each day a different sentry will stand guard," Swift Horse said, nodding down at Marsha, then again looking at his warriors. He stopped at Sharp Nose. "Your day is now."

Sharp Nose nodded.

They all filed out of the cave, Sharp Nose with them, then he went on away from them to find the perfect place for watching the cave's entrance.

Swift Horse, Marsha, and the others rode in silence to the village. As Marsha stepped into her cabin, from the back door she smelled something familiar to her, then realized it was coming from the kitchen. Soft Wind was preparing the evening meal.

"Marsha? Is that you?" Soft Wind called from the kitchen.

"Yes, it is I," Marsha said, removing her leather jacket and hanging it from a peg on the wall.

She pulled the damp ribbon from her hair and hung it on another peg, then removed her gloves, and thankfully her boots. Now that they were wet, they were too snug. It felt good to be able to wiggle her toes again.

Soft Wind came from the kitchen wearing an apron with evident splatters of tomato sauce on it, proof that she still wasn't all that comfortable making dishes that until recently had been unknown to her.

That made Marsha smile, for it did seem strange to see someone dressed in doeskin wearing something of the white world, especially from the kitchen.

"What did you find?" Soft Wind asked, drying her hands on the tail end of the apron.

"The trunk that Swift Horse saw in his vision," Marsha murmured, going and hugging Soft Wind. Then, being chilled through and through, she went and stood before the fireplace, soaking up its warmth.

"Did my brother take the trunk from the cave?" Soft Wind asked, coming to stand beside Marsha.

Marsha turned to her and wearily explained Swift Horse's plan. Little did she know that at that moment One Eye would be planning yet another murder—that of Sharp Nose.

Chapter 32

Look in thy glass, and tell the face thou viewest
Now is the time that face should form another. . . .
—William Shakespeare

One Eye smiled to himself as he sat on his horse, a bow slung across his shoulder, a quiver of arrows at his back. He had left the cave only long enough to get a drink from the river when he had heard the sound of horses approaching in the distance.

One Eye had had only enough time to reach the other side of the river and hide.

"Swift Horse," he had whispered to himself as he watched Swift Horse and the others ride back in the direction of Swift Horse's village after having all been in the cave.

"And the woman," he said aloud, bitterly. Even she had been with Swift Horse and his warriors.

Ever since she had arrived at the village, she had been all things bad for One Eye. She had begun taking up valuable time with Swift Horse that had usually been One Eye's time with his friend. And now that she had agreed to marry Swift Horse, One Eye had known that there would be no time, ever again, for two old friends to get together to talk, laugh, and discuss old times.

And the woman would not rest until she had made Swift Horse believe it was One Eye who was, in truth, the one-eyed renegade.

"Her time on this earth is measured now in heartbeats, for soon she will die," he said, riding alongside the river in the direction of the cave, yet back far enough from the riverbank so that Sharp Nose could not see him.

He rode onward until he knew that he was out of eye range of Sharp Nose, then crossed over at a shallow place in the river. When he was on the other side, he directed his steed to the back side of the cave, where he knew Sharp Nose still stood, alert and watchful.

Even though One Eye knew this sentry very well, and they had shared many smokes and talks, One Eye had to kill him in order to go inside the cave and get the trunk. One Eye had to do away with it once and for all, for as long as it was where someone could find it, it could be used against him.

First he must do away with the trunk—although he was proud of the valuables that he had placed there—and then he must do away with the woman.

But there was still one problem: the scar on his head! The injury was still plain to see, but he would not carry that scar forever, the way he had been forced to carry the one following the bear attack.

His shaman had been applying his medicinal cure on the wound on his head, and the scar left there was all but gone. What was visible, was hidden behind medicine that was the same color as his skin. The shaman had told him this morning that in only a day or two the scar would no longer be visible at all to the naked eye.

If One Eye could wait just that amount of time before going to Swift Horse's village, then he could stand before Swift Horse without fearing being detected as the renegade. Before then, though, he had to find a way to finally end the woman's life.

Now close enough to Sharp Nose that he could see his back, and seeing that Sharp Nose's horse was tethered far away, One Eye drew a tight rein and dismounted. He did not need to go any farther. He was accurate with his bow and arrow.

One arrow was all that he needed to silence Sharp Nose, and then he could go and take the trunk to the river and drop it into the deepest depths so that no one would ever see it again.

After securing his horse's reins, One Eye drew an arrow from his quiver, positioned it on the string of his bow, and took aim.

The arrow quickly found its place in the right side of Sharp Nose's back. Thinking that he had no need to go and verify that Sharp Nose was dead, One Eye slung his bow across his shoulder again, mounted his steed, then rode on to the cave.

He tethered his horse to a low tree limb, then went into the cave and hurried to the rear where the trunk stood, now open.

He could tell that someone had rifled through it and had seen all of the personal belongings of those who had died at One Eye's hand. He slammed the trunk closed and carried it to the cave's entrance.

He lifted it high over his head and slung it through the falls, watching it tumble along with the falling waters until it splashed far down below him in deep enough water to keep it hidden from anyone's view, forever.

Then he grabbed all of the torches from the cave walls and pitched them into the water too.

He turned and gazed behind him at the darkness, laughing at how clever he was to have destroyed all evidence against him, then walked from the cave and made his way across the tiny, slippery ledge.

He hurried to his horse and, laughing into the wind, rode away, his thoughts already on how he would end the woman's life. And if he discovered that Swift Horse had finally believed her about his being the guilty party, he would have no choice but to also take Swift Horse's life—and anyone else who pointed an accusing finger at Chief One Eye.

He was too clever for them all.

He started to make a sharp right turn to head in the direction of his village, hoping to avoid everyone until his new scar was invisible, but drew a quick, tight rein when he saw someone at the river, fishing.

"The black man called Abraham," he said, his lips lifting into a wicked grin.

He sank his heels into the flanks of his steed and rode toward him, stopping when Abraham turned and saw him there. He could tell that Abraham was uneasy from seeing him and wondered if he knew the doubts others had about the sort of person he was.

"Abraham, my friend," One Eye said, dismounting.

Abraham took an unsteady step away from One Eye, then tripped.

One Eye stood menacingly over him, his one eye filled with pure evil as he stared down at him.

Chapter 33

Beauty is but a vain and doubtful good;
A shining gloss that vadeth suddenly;
A flower that dies when first it 'gins to bud. . . .
— William Shakespeare

Just before reaching their village, Swift Horse looked quickly toward the river. He just now remembered having promised Abraham that he would go fishing with him today. Abraham had voiced his love of catfish.

Since Abraham deserved those special moments that freedom now allowed him, Swift Horse had decided never to let him down. And he had! With the dream so strong on his mind this morning, all else had been forgotten.

He turned to Marsha. "I must go and find Abraham and apologize to him," he said, drawing a tight rein as his warriors rode onward without him. "I promised that I would go fishing with him today, but in the flurry of needing to get to the cave, I forgot. I had already given

Abraham fishing gear, and we were supposed to meet at the river after the morning meal."

"Do you think he's there even now waiting on you?" Marsha asked, gazing toward the river but seeing no one there. "I don't see him."

"I will ride on down to the river and see if I find him," Swift Horse answered. "Maybe he is searching even now for a better place to fish."

"I'll go with you," Marsha volunteered. She smiled at Swift Horse. "I'm not quite ready to leave you yet, for I know that when you get home, you will go into council with your warriors."

"Yes, we must discuss what we will do next if One Eye doesn't come for the trunk," Swift Horse said solemnly.

"It is so good to hear you speak so," Marsha said. "I thought you would never believe that he is the one guilty of these terrible crimes."

"I still want him to step into a trap of his own doing rather than my going to and accusing him in front of his people," Swift Horse said, his voice drawn. "His people do not deserve a leader such as he. Some will even find it hard to believe, as I have."

He turned with a start when Sharp Nose's son, Four Leaves, came running toward him, carrying a fishing pole.

"I was walking beside the river and found this, and there is fishing equipment spilled where I found it," Four Leaves said, holding the pole out before him. "My chief, is this pole not yours?"

Swift Horse's heart skipped a beat when he saw that it was the one that he had given to Abraham.

"Yes, this is mine," he said, then looked past Four Leaves. "Take me to where you found it. Did you not see Abraham near where you found it? And you said that you found spilled fishing equipment?"

"I have not seen Abraham at all this morning," Four Leaves said, shrugging. He pointed to the place where he had found the pole and the equipment, then looked up at Swift Horse again. "Over there. That is where I found the pole. That is where I saw the equipment."

Swift Horse sank his heels into the flanks of his steed and rode hard toward the river, Marsha close behind him. When they came to where Swift Horse assumed Abraham had been, Swift Horse leaped from his horse, bent to a knee, and studied the footprints in the sand.

"There has been a scuffle here," Swift Horse said, seeing the large prints made by the moccasins that had been given to Abraham, and then

saw prints made by someone other than the
young brave. He could tell that Abraham had
struggled with the one who came up on him
while he was fishing, but had lost the struggle.
His footprints led away with whoever had
forced him to go with him.

He started to follow the tracks, which included those of a horse, but stopped when he
saw Sharp Nose riding toward him, barely able
to sit in his saddle. He was slumped over, and
slid slowly from side to side, his head hanging.

"Sharp Nose!" Swift Horse gasped out, then
ran to him just as his friend fell from the horse.

The warrior fell onto his side on the ground,
his eyes wild as Swift Horse stood over him staring at the arrow lodged in the right side of his
back, blood streaming from it.

"It . . . was . . . One Eye. . . ." Sharp Nose
gasped out as Swift Horse knelt beside him,
stunned that Sharp Nose was even still alive.

"One . . . Eye . . . thought I was dead," Sharp
Nose managed to say in a whisper. He looked
past his chief and saw his son, Four Leaves, running toward them, panic in his eyes to see his father downed in such a way.

Sharp Nose looked quickly at his chief again.
"I watched as One Eye got the trunk and threw it
from the cave, down into the water below the

falls." He reached a hand out for Swift Horse and grabbed him by a wrist. "A short while later, as I was coming this way, I . . . was . . . close enough to see One Eye leading Abraham . . . through the forest," he said, his voice getting so low, Swift Horse could scarcely hear him now.

"He . . . they . . . did not see me."

Swift Horse was grateful to realize that Marsha had ridden away, surely to get Bright Moon, in hopes of saving this proud warrior. Four Leaves knelt now beside his father, tears streaming from his eyes.

"You said that you saw him with Abraham?" Swift Horse asked, bringing Sharp Nose's eyes back to him.

"One . . . Eye . . . was leading him into the forest at knifepoint, trailing his horse behind him," Sharp Nose said, then closed his eyes and said nothing more.

"*Ahte*, Father!" Four Leaves cried, then looked pleadingly at Swift Horse. "Do . . . something. . . ."

Distress filled Swift Horse at thinking that he might lose a valiant warrior at the hands of so evil a man as One Eye.

"Sharp Nose, do not die," Swift Horse said, his voice breaking. "Bright Moon will soon be here." Just as he said that, Bright Moon came running toward them, his parfleche medicine bag in his right hand, his long gray hair trailing behind him.

"Is he in time?" Marsha asked as she ran up beside Swift Horse. She blanched when she saw the stillness of Sharp Nose and the fear in his son's eyes. "No! Please don't let him be dead."

"He is barely breathing, but he had enough breath to tell me everything he saw. Abraham has been taken away by One Eye," Swift Horse said, rising and making room for Bright Moon, who was quickly on his haunches beside Sharp Nose.

Marsha gasped and looked away as Bright Moon broke the arrow shaft in half and tossed it aside, the rest still lodged in the warrior's back.

"He still lives," Bright Moon said, then began his ritual of chanting as he applied medicines around the wound. "I need to take him home. I cannot do all that needs to be done here, away from the fire. I must heat instruments to remove the rest of the arrow."

Instantly several warriors ran up, ready to assist. They picked Sharp Nose up and began carrying him toward the village, Bright Moon and Four Leaves walking with them.

Marsha and Swift Horse were alone now, gazing into the dark shadows of the forest where they knew Abraham had been taken.

"If he kills Abraham . . ." Swift Horse said from between clenched teeth, his hands tight fists at his sides. "If he does, the death will be on my hands, not One Eye's, because I should have believed earlier that One Eye was the one guilty of the crimes you accused him of."

He turned and gazed at his warriors as they took Sharp Nose on into the village. "His death, too," he said, his voice breaking.

Marsha took him by a hand. "Do not do this to yourself," she urged. "You wanted to believe in someone, and not just someone—a friend. I understand how you wouldn't want to believe that he could do these things. He has been a friend for so long."

"How could I have not seen the signs?" Swift Horse said, gazing down at Marsha.

"Because you did not want to," she said, reaching a comforting hand to his cheek. "But now you must think of Abraham. His life is in danger."

Edward James came running toward them, his eyes filled with fear. He waved frantically at them with both of his hands.

"What now?" Marsha said, seeing the fear in her brother's eyes.

"It's Soft Wind!" Edward James said, stopping when he reached them, breathless. "She left a short while ago with some other women to gather roots. It was such a beautiful morning, she was so eager to go. When I heard about Sharp Nose, and Abraham . . . I could not help but be concerned about the welfare of my wife and those women who are with her."

A sharp panic entered Swift Horse's heart. He turned and stared again into the forest, and then at Edward James. "How long have they been gone?" he asked.

"Too long," Edward James said, wringing his hands. "When I saw Sharp Nose being brought back in such a condition and I was told what happened, all I could think about was my wife and those who left with her. What if One Eye comes upon them as they are digging their roots? Will he kill them? Or remember they are friends?"

"He is a madman, so it is impossible to know what he would do," Swift Horse said, already in his saddle.

"I want to go, too," Marsha said, stepping into the stirrup, and soon in her saddle.

"This is becoming too dangerous," Swift Horse said, frowning at Marsha. "Please stay with your brother."

"Stay?" Edward James said, his eyes wide. "I can't stay. I've got to go with you."

"Let me have your horse, Marsha," Edward James said, already grabbing the reins. "You stay behind. Lord, Marsha, I don't want you in danger, too."

"You have no idea how much I've already experienced today, so believe me, big brother, I am going with you," Marsha said stubbornly.

She looked over at Sharp Nose's horse, then at her brother as she yanked her reins from him. "Take Sharp Nose's steed," she suggested.

Edward James gave her a frenzied look, then hurried into Sharp Nose's saddle.

"We will follow the tracks made by One Eye and Abraham, for then we will know whether or not they encountered the women," Swift Horse said, already riding off in a soft lope as he gazed down at the tracks. Marsha and Edward James stayed back from him, yet close together.

"Marsha, I wish you'd reconsider and go home," Edward James said, giving her a pleading look.

"I want to help if I can," she murmured, yet understood the true danger and knew that her brother was terribly worried about her.

"You have always been so stubborn," he said, then looked ahead as they rode onward behind Swift Horse.

"I wonder why One Eye took Abraham?" Marsha blurted out.

"Because One Eye knows that Abraham is Swift Horse's friend—a friend he might have believed was taking One Eye's place in Swift Horse's life," Edward James said, trying to rationalize all of this in his mind, yet hardly able to think of anything or anyone but his wife.

"So it's because of jealousy?" Marsha asked, her eyebrows forking.

"It might be because of revenge," Edward James said thickly. "If Abraham is killed, One Eye knows it will cause pain inside Swift Horse's heart. Now he seems only to want to inflict pain—pain on Swift Horse, for he has to know that he can no longer hide who he is from anyone, especially Swift Horse."

"I just wish it was over," Marsha said, her voice breaking. "I'm so afraid someone else is going to die, and it might not be One Eye."

Edward James gave her a wavering glance, then followed Swift Horse farther and farther into the forest.

Chapter 34

My first thought was, he lied in every word. . . .
—Robert Browning

One Eye had almost reached his tethered horse with Abraham walking ahead of him, a knife ready if he tried to escape, when he saw something so tempting he just could not fail to take advantage of it.

On a slight slope of land, Soft Wind and a friend were on their knees, digging roots.

He looked past them, and saw other women doing the same, farther away.

But Soft Wind and her friend were isolated enough from the others for One Eye to get more vengeance against his longtime friend—who was now his enemy.

He would kill his sister!

He would kill the woman with her, as well!

It gave him a dark pleasure to see the fear in

the black man's eyes that he knew that he would soon die and no one would be there to do anything about it. When Swift Horse found his sister and then later, Abraham, it would be enough vengeance put upon him by a one-eyed man— a man who had been a friend for so long.

Anger raced like a hot flash of fire through him when he thought of the day of the bear attack. Swift Horse was not worthy of such a sacrifice. If he were, he would fight to save One Eye from the fate that now awaited him, and would never believe anyone who pointed an accusing finger at One Eye.

First he would kill the women, and then he would kill Abraham, and then it would be done and over with.

He would wait for Swift Horse, and just as Swift Horse came close enough to One Eye, the hate and the need for vengeance visible in his eyes, One Eye would kill himself as Swift Horse looked on. One Eye's last act to make the hurt run more deeply within Swift Horse was to see the man he had loved as a friend kill himself. His only regret was that he had not killed Marsha, too.

Needing to secure Abraham before attempting to kill the two women, he gave Abraham a shove. "Hurry onward," he said in a quiet yet threatening command. "You see my horse. Hurry to it."

Abraham did as he was told, his knees visibly trembling, and when he did reach the horse, he was grabbed and shoved against a tree.

"You stay there," One Eye growled out. "If you try to run, I throw an accurate knife. You think the pain of your wounds made by a whip were bad, you will not know true pain until a knife slams into your body."

"I won't go nowhere," Abraham said, his eyes wide as he watched the one-eyed man go to his horse and take a rope from the bag that hung at the horse's right side.

"Are you gonna hang me?" Abraham gasped raspily as One Eye uncoiled the rope and walked toward him with it. One Eye's only response was a guttural laugh.

He used the rope to secure Abraham to the tree.

One Eye stood before Abraham as he yanked his knife from the sheath at his right side. "If you cry out for help, I will not kill you instantly when I return, I will kill you slowly and painfully."

Abraham visibly trembled, the rope cutting into his flesh where it held him in place against the tree.

One Eye glared at him, then ran stealthily toward the clearing.

Just as he got there and was poised to plunge the knife into Soft Wind's chest, a gun blast rang out.

One Eye felt an instant sting in his belly and realized that he had just been shot. He dropped his knife and grabbed at his stomach, feeling the heat of blood as it seeped between his fingers.

Just as his knees buckled beneath him, he saw Swift Horse step out into the open, smoke spiraling upward from the barrel of his rifle.

"You . . ." One Eye gasped, now on his knees, blinking his one eye over and over again as he fought off dying. "Swift Horse, you . . . would . . . do this . . . ?"

Swift Horse felt a keen remorse intermingled with pangs of hate as he watched One Eye's lone eye close and One Eye topple over onto his stomach, headfirst.

Marsha ran to Swift Horse's side as Edward James gathered Soft Wind into his arms.

"He . . . was going . . . to kill me," Soft Wind gulped out, clinging hard to her husband. "One Eye *was* the one-eyed renegade."

"Yes, he was guilty all along and I was too blinded to see it," Swift Horse said, dropping his rifle to the ground. He hung his head in his hands. "Because of me, because of my faith in that man, many had to suffer."

"I found Abraham," a voice rang out as one of Swift Horse's warriors found Abraham tied to the tree. "He is all right."

That news came to Swift Horse like a breath of fresh air, because if Abraham had died, Swift Horse might not have forgiven himself.

"It's over now," Marsha reassured, as Swift Horse looked at her with an apologetic gaze. "Please don't feel guilty for anything that has to do with One Eye. You were a dedicated, loyal friend, who just did not want to believe there was evil in your longtime friend."

"You did what only a true friend would do," Edward James said, walking up closer to Swift Horse and Marsha, Soft Wind at his side, his arm around her waist. "You believed in a friend and your friendship."

Abraham came toward Swift Horse, smiling broadly. "I am all right," he said, reassuring Swift Horse that he was. "The ropes were tight on me, but tha's all. I'm alive. But had you not come . . ."

"Let's not think about what-if's," Marsha said, giving Abraham a soft smile. "Let's just thank the Lord that that man's evil has been silenced forever."

The other women who had walked farther away from Soft Wind and her friend came running toward them, baskets in hand, their eyes wide with fear. When they saw One Eye lying there, stilled by a bullet in his belly, they stopped and stared down at him, then gazed up at Swift Horse with questioning in their eyes.

"He was evil, through and through," Swift Horse said thickly. He gazed down at One Eye. "But he was not always that way." He swallowed hard. "I believe the day the bear attacked him and took away one of his eyes was the day that One Eye changed. For so long he could not look at his reflection in the mirror of the river water, for he was ashamed of how he looked. I tried to reassure him by telling him that everyone looked past those scars and saw, instead, his inner self, which was good. But he could not get past how the women looked away from him in disgust since that day. There was no changing that."

"I feel to blame," Soft Wind said, a sob lodging in the depths of her throat. "I knew that he cared deeply for me, yet I did not love him even before his accident."

"Never blame yourself for any of this," Edward James said, placing his hands at his wife's shoulders and turning her to face him. "He is what he made himself to be. There had to have been something in him long before that day of the bear's attack for him to have become so evil. He was born evil, but just did not allow anyone to see it."

"I do recall how sometimes, when we were very young braves who had only small bows to carry around with us, he would shoot tiny forest animals with his arrow when only moments before he and I had been playing with them," Swift Horse said, his voice breaking. "It would always be when my back was turned and he would then say that it was an accident, knowing that I could not say otherwise."

"Let's go," Marsha urged, taking Swift Horse by a hand. "Let's put this behind us, for always. We have more important things to think about— like our marriage. Now that this is behind us, we can finally have our ceremony." She smiled up at him. "Can we tomorrow?" she rushed out. "Wouldn't that be a wonderful thing to make you forget today?"

"I shall never forget today, nor that it was I who killed someone who has been a part of my life since I was but a small brave, even as far back as when we took our first steps together," Swift Horse said.

He took his hands from hers, turned his back

to One Eye, then nodded. "Yes, let us get this behind us," he said. He turned to Marsha. "But I have one more thing to do, first."

"That is?" Marsha asked, yet knew almost for certain what he was referring to.

"I must go and tell One Eye's people about him, as well as take his body to them," Swift Horse said, a shiver racing across his flesh to know that he must have those last moments with someone he had never truly known. He did have to take him home.

"Can't someone else do it?" Marsha asked, searching his eyes.

"It is my responsibility," Swift Horse said thickly.

He turned to his warriors. "Place him on his horse," he said, nodding toward One Eye. "Accompany me to his village."

"Abraham and I will take the women home," Edward James said, smiling over at Abraham, who quickly nodded in agreement.

Swift Horse nodded, then he went to Marsha and took her hands in his. "Tomorrow is ours," he said, bending and brushing a kiss across her brow.

She gazed adoringly into his eyes. "Yes, ours . . ." she murmured, then watched him leave with One Eye's body, stifling a sob behind her hand.

"We've a wedding to get ready for," Edward James said, trying to lighten everyone's mood. "Come on, little sister, we've much to do."

"I'll stay with the women to keep them safe," Abraham said as the women gathered around him.

Marsha gave Abraham a smile, then saddled her steed as Edward James placed Soft Wind on his horse, her basket of roots being carried by one of the women.

Chapter 35

My perfect wife . . .
Oh heart, my own, oh eyes, mine too. . . .
                                        —Robert Browning

Several years later

It was a warm day of spring, when new sprouts were appearing on the trees, and flowers were just pushing their way through the earth that had been watered most of the winter by snow.

Robins warbled in the trees near the Creek village. At the nearby river, and even in the creeks that dissected the land near the Creek village, an occasional eager fish leaped from the water, seemingly glad that the ice was no longer there to hinder its movements.

The sun was brilliant overhead in a blue sky, where only occasional puffs of white clouds scudded past.

Marsha had learned that the "chunkey yard"

was an integral part of the Creek village. The yard where the game was played was continually swept clean and was often surrounded by banks of earth from the repeated sweeping.

"Come on, son!" Marsha shouted as she sat beside her husband amidst their Wind Clan, cheering on their ten-year-old son Moon Thunder as he played chunkey with friends of his same age. "Come on, Moon Thunder! You can win!"

She heard a chuckle beside her and turned to find Swift Horse watching her, having always admired her enthusiasm for games his people played—especially if her husband or son, or even her nephew, were among those who were competing.

"Am I too loud again?" Marsha asked, blushing when she looked over her shoulder to see if her cheers had brought attention of others away from the game and to her.

"No, my wife, you are not too loud," Swift Horse said, sliding an arm around her waist and drawing her up next to him. "It is good to see you so proud of our son."

"I'm as proud of our daughter," Marsha said. Soft Wind was babysitting the children today. Marsha's niece Sweet Butterfly would spend the afternoon playing dolls with her daughter Pretty Sky.

She turned again toward those who were competing in the game, among them not only Swift Horse's and Marsha's son, but also Soft Wind and Edward James's.

Edward James and Soft Wind had chosen to name one child with an Indian name, the other with one that was used in the white community—especially since their son had hardly any outward appearances of being part Creek. Everything about him was Edward James all over again!

Edward James knew of the prejudices of white people toward those whose skin was red, and he had big plans for his son Jimmy. He was going to see that he had the best schooling, and even now Jimmy attended school at the closest town, Paducah.

But it wasn't only schooling that he planned for his son. He wanted him to have a college education. Jimmy had voiced his desire to be a lawyer—someone who could fight for the rights of the red man.

His goals were quite different from Moon Thunder's. Once Moon Thunder had completed his education, he wanted to return to his people and teach those children whose parents would not allow them to attend school where whites attended.

Moon Thunder had looked past ridicule that some whites were guilty of during his time at school. He had a future to look toward and he would not allow anyone to get in his way!

Also, he knew that one day he would step into his father's footsteps as chief of their Wind Clan. How better to become a great a leader than to get an education that would help him know how to stand up against white people who would try to take the freedom away from their Wind Clan of Creek? Moon Thunder had said that between him and Jimmy, with their knowledge of so many things, no one would ever get the best of their people!

"We have been blessed with a wonderful daughter and son, that is true," Swift Horse said, nodding. "As I have been blessed with a wonderful wife."

"Our life—" Marsha started to say, but when she heard her son let out a loud whooping sound, she turned quickly, just in time to see his spear land the closest to the place where the chunkey stone had stopped, meaning he was the victor this time.

The first time she had seen this game played, was when Swift Horse had played it with his

warriors. She had watched intensely as the play-
ers rolled a stone disk and then attempted to es-
timate where the stone would stop rolling. The
object was to see who could land his spear the
closest to the place the chunkey stone had
stopped, as Moon Thunder had just done.

Cheers rang into the air as all those who had
been in competition with Moon Thunder circled
around him, patting him on the back and con-
gratulating him. And then just as quickly the
competition began again.

"As you know, this can go on for many more
hours," Swift Horse said as he drew Marsha's
eyes back to him. "I do not believe our sons will
miss us should we leave and take a walk along
the river. I might even pluck you a bouquet for
your kitchen table."

"Now, how can I say no to such a proposition
as that?" Marsha said, laughing softly.

When she and Swift Horse reached the river,
they stopped and gazed across it, at how gentle
it was today, and beautiful with the weeping wil-
lows hanging down over it in places, with their
fresh growth of leaves on their swaying limbs.

"Everything is new and fresh," Marsha murmured. She inhaled a deep breath of the midafternoon air. "I love spring."

"Even though I will soon be gone for several

days as I join my warriors on the hunt for the white-tailed deer?" Swift Horse said, turning her to face him. He gazed into her eyes. "I want to bring home much meat for my family, and pelts that can be made into beautiful clothes that you are now so skilled at making."

"I love sewing, especially with beads," Marsha murmured.

She glanced over her shoulder at her brother's store, knowing that he was there even now, preparing his shelves for the arrival of fresh pelts. He always showed such enthusiasm this time of year, for his trading post was now known wide and far, a favorite of all who were based in Kentucky.

"Edward James is missing the game today," she murmured. "But he has seen our sons participate enough times during the nontrading season."

"And he has even participated a time or two," Swift Horse said, chuckling. "It is good to compete with him in that way. He has become quite a chunkey player, you know."

"Yes, I know," Marsha said, now walking hand-in-hand with Swift Horse beside the river, farther away from the village.

Suddenly a deer ran past, then came back and

playfully nuzzled Marsha's hand as she held it out for her.

"Abraham has to be more careful with Sandy now that hunting season is near," she said, now stooping and hugging the beautiful, grown deer that seemed to believe it was human, not animal.

It was a pet, that was for sure, yet too large now to live in the cabin with Abraham. Abraham had built Sandy her own cabin behind his, where much straw had been placed for the deer to sleep upon, and for warmth.

"Sandy!" Abraham shouted as he came running toward Marsha and Swift Horse, his eyes on the deer. "Sandy, you're getting too frisky for this ol' black man."

"Good morning, Abraham," Marsha said, smiling at him as he came and stopped, the deer soon nuzzling his hand, then standing close beside him as Abraham petted her.

"Mornin', ma'am," Abraham said, still panting from having run so hard to catch up with his pet deer. He gazed over at Swift Horse. "Mornin', Swift Horse," he said, smiling broadly. "I saw your son win the game of chunkey twice now today."

He looked past them as the game continued, then smiled at Marsha. "I saw your brother's boy win, too," he said. "Both boys are skilled at the game." He bowed his head, then looked up again with sadness in his eyes. "I had a son once," he said. "He would've been a good chunkey game player."

"Yes, I'm sure he would have," Marsha said, always feeling so deeply for this man and what he had gone through in his life. But since he had become a part of the Creek's life, life had been good and loving for him.

"Abraham, you know the hunt begins soon," Swift Horse said, gazing at the deer and then at Abraham. "Times like this, when Sandy gets away from you, can end in tragedy."

"I know," Abraham said, then nodded. "I plan to take Sandy home and make certain she doesn't get loose again. My heart would break if anything happened to my pet."

"Mine too," Marsha murmured, reaching a hand to Sandy and gently stroking her. She had been with Abraham the two times he had planned to set the animal free but had been, in the end, unable to do it. And she understood. She loved the animal almost as much as it were human!

"The animal is so adorable," she murmured.

"I'll be seein' you two soon again," Abraham said, turning and walking away from them, Sandy at his heels.

"As fond as he is of that animal, I don't doubt that he'll keep a close watch on her now," Marsha said, then began walking again with Swift Horse. "I will miss you so much when you are gone on the hunt."

"As I will miss you," Swift Horse said, smiling over at her. "As I always have when we are apart."

"I love the winters so much," Marsha murmured. "You are home most of the time. It is good to have you with me while I bake, sew, and play with our daughter."

"She, too, will one day be school age," Swift Horse said. "Are you certain you will send her to a white school, or teach her yourself, as you did before our son asked to go to school with Jimmy?"

"I'm not sure yet," Marsha said, sighing. "I still have time to think about it. She is only three."

"Our marriage is a good one," Swift Horse said, stopping and placing his hands at Marsha's shoulders, turning her to face him. "I will never forget the day we spoke our vows, how beautiful you were, how my people accepted you so quickly."

"I think of that day often, too," Marsha murmured, even now catapulted back in time, remembering how gently and sweetly Swift Horse had treated her during the ceremony.

And, ah, how handsome he had been!

He had worn a scarlet cloak trimmed in fur, and his thick hair, also intertwined with fur, had hung in one long braid down his back. All of this matched the fur he wore around his neck that denoted him as chief of his Wind Clan. But it had been the sheath of eagle feathers that he had carried that day—and how he had presented it to her—that had been the most special.

It was mainly what he said that clung to her, making her heart soar each time she remembered his words: "These are the feathers of the eagle, which is the swiftest of birds," he had said to her. "These feathers are a sign of my love for you—my devotion, forever and ever."

That sheath of feathers now hung on the wall just above their bed, where she could see it every night before she went to sleep with her beloved husband, and each morning as she awakened to a brand-new day with Swift Horse.

After their vows had been exchanged and they had been blessed by Bright Moon, they had joined their people for a village-wide dance and a feast of bear's ribs barbecued with honey.

The height of her wonder at this special day had come when she had danced around the outdoor fire with her husband as everyone watched—their eyes expressing happiness and peace . . . such a pride for their beloved chief.

From that moment onward she knew that she was truly accepted by his people as one of them; as one *with* them.

Loud cheers behind her at the chunkey yard broke through her reverie. She turned and gazed in that direction, then looked at her husband with questioning in her eyes. "I wonder who won this time?" she murmured.

"Let us go and see," Swift Horse said, turning with Marsha, both walking briskly back toward their village to where the game was being played. They were so proud of their son and nephew as they challenged each other as to who was the better player of the game.

When they arrived at the chunkey yard, they saw that neither their son nor nephew won this time. Sharp Nose's son Long Nose had won. He was their same age, a son who came after Sharp Nose's complete recovery after having been downed by One Eye's arrow that terrible day.

His other son, Four Leaves, was away from the village, married to a woman of another clan—the Wolf Clan, which had at one time had One Eye as its chief.

Once One Eye was gone, another chief was

named, and it was that chief's daughter who had fallen in love with Four Leaves after she had come with her father to check on the health of Sharp Nose as he recovered from the arrow wound.

It had been love at first sight, although both children were not of the age they could marry.

"Our son and nephew can't win every time," Marsha said, laughing softly. She turned with Swift Horse and walked toward their home. "Now let's go see how our daughter and niece are faring," she murmured.

Life for them all was good and without the interference of whites.

Fort Hill was no longer active.

Those who had been there, had been stationed elsewhere.

As it was, the Creek warriors could enjoy their hunts, and the women could enjoy their lives of being wives and mothers.

Marsha couldn't see how it could have been any other way for her. The day her father had decided to move to Kentucky had been fateful on one hand, and wonderful on the other, for had they not come to Kentucky, she would have never met and married such a wonderful man as Swift Horse, nor would she be the mother of two such beautiful children.

She had hopes of having more children one day, but for now she was content with what God had blessed her with!

A husband, two children, a loving sister-in-law, and a big brother who never ceased to amaze her at how adoring he was to her.

No, she could never ask for more than this!

Dear Reader:

I hope you enjoyed reading *Swift Horse*. The next book in my Signet Indian series is *Running Fox*. It is filled with much excitement, romance, mystery, and adventure. *Running Fox* will be in stores in December 2006.

Many of you say that you are collecting my Indian romances. For my entire backlist of books, or for information about my fan club, you can send for my latest newsletter and autographed bookmark. For an assured reply, please send a stamped, self-addressed, legal-sized envelope to:

Cassie Edwards
6709 North Country Club Road
Mattoon, IL 61938

Thank you for your support of my Indian series. I love researching and writing about our Native Americans! I aspire to write about every major tribe in America!

Always,

Cassie Edwards
www.cassieedwards.com